'Maybe it was before.'

'I doubt it,' Nicole replied. 'My twin is six feet tall, a captain in the army. . .and he also has a moustache.'

Matthew stared at her for a long moment, then he threw back his head and laughed. 'Maybe you have a double,' he said.

'Are you one of those people that thinks everyone has a twin or a double?'

'Not necessarily.' His eyes gleamed with amusement. 'I do sometimes wonder if everyone doesn't have a soul-mate and if that isn't instantly recognisable. . .but that's another thing altogether.'

Laura MacDonald lives in the Isle of Wight. She is married and has a grown-up family. She has enjoyed writing fiction since she was a child, but for several years she worked for members of the medical profession, both in pharmacy and in general practice. Her daughter is a nurse and has helped with the research for Laura's medical stories.

Recent titles by the same author:

IN AT THE DEEP END
STRICTLY PROFESSIONAL
TO LOVE AGAIN
FALSE IMPRESSIONS
SOMEBODY TO LOVE

THE DECIDING FACTOR

BY

LAURA MACDONALD

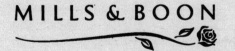

MILLS & BOON

*All the characters in this book have no existence outside the
imagination of the author, and have no relation whatsoever to anyone
bearing the same name or names. They are not even distantly inspired
by any individual known or unknown to the author, and all the
incidents are pure invention.*

*MILLS & BOON, the Rose Device and LOVE ON CALL
are trademarks of the publisher.*
Harlequin Mills & Boon Limited,
Eton House, 18–24 Paradise Road, Richmond, Surrey TW9 1SR
*This edition published by arrangement with
Harlequin Enterprises B.V.*

© Laura MacDonald 1995

ISBN 0 263 79095 9

*Set in 10½ on 12 pt Linotron Times
03-9506-49581*

*Typeset in Great Britain by CentraCet, Cambridge
Made and printed in Great Britain*

CHAPTER ONE

IT WAS one of those moments; a million to one chance meeting, sudden recognition in the glance of a stranger.

Later, Nicole wondered if it had been love at first sight, but that was much later, after all the anguish and uncertainty. . .and besides, at the time she didn't believe in such things. Even if she had, a bookshop in the heart of town on a hot Saturday afternoon in August would be the last place she would expect it to happen.

She had been browsing quite happily in the travel section, on the point of moving on to new fiction, which she had been saving until last, when she had become aware of someone on the other side of the stand. She had looked up at the precise moment that he did—their eyes had met, recognition flared and sudden pleasure surged inside her.

'Hello!' she began, then stopped in sudden confusion as his spontaneous smile also faded and a puzzled frown creased his forehead.

'I'm sorry,' he said at last, 'I thought I knew you.'

'Me too.' She smiled again, relieved that he had apparently made the same mistake.

'Have we met before?' The frown was still there as he sought to recall.

'I don't think so. . .' she said slowly. She knew now that they hadn't met. . .but for one moment there. . .

'Do you live here?' His voice was deep, slightly husky, his eyes dark like his hair. . .his face, not handsome in the accepted sense of the word, but the features strong, clean-cut.

He was older that she, probably forties, she thought, the hair at the temples greying slightly.

'Yes——' she took a deep breath '—but only just— a week, that's all.'

'Ah.' He raised dark eyebrows. 'Then you must have a twin.'

She smiled. 'Maybe I have.'

He nodded but didn't immediately move away, lingering, as if reluctant to go, reluctant to destroy the moment.

In the end it was a small child in a buggy claiming his mother's attention who broke the spell, and the man moved away, then hesitated and glanced briefly back at Nicole.

'Goodbye.' He smiled once more, then he was gone, out of the shop, to be swallowed up in the crowd of afternoon shoppers.

She sighed, wondering for one moment about the apparent intensity of the incident, then she too moved on, but by then the new fiction had somehow lost its appeal.

Petrol fumes spewed into the sultry atmosphere and the heat rose from the road in a shimmering haze as Nicole slowly made her way out of the shopping precinct and crossed the bridge over the river.

There was an air of lethargy about the shoppers who trailed home heavily laden with supermarket carrier-bags, while on the riverbank little groups sprawled lazily on the dry parched grass: families seeking a shady spot beneath the willows, children feeding the ducks, or young couples entwined in each other's arms.

Nicole paused for a moment to watch a barge brightly painted in green and red and gaudily decorated with flowers as it entered the lock beside the bridge. Its owner was throwing a rope to a boy who ran alongside on the towpath, while a small white terrier barked furiously from the deck.

Leaving the bridge, she began to climb the steep, cobbled road that wound and twisted out of the town. On one side were the ruins of a medieval castle that stood guard over the sprawl of shops and houses below, and on the other, a large park, its huge trees a mantle of greens and copper covering the soft mossy darkness of lawns and neatly tended flowerbeds.

Hawksford was a lovely old town and Nicole was becoming more pleased by the day that she had come here to live and to work.

She'd had her doubts at first, doubts about leaving her previous job and the friends she had made, but on the whole it had been a sensible move. Her mother was not in good health, and the journey from Stockport to her home in Portchester on the south coast had become too arduous for Nicole to make too often.

When the post of senior staff midwife on the obstetric unit at the Spencer Rathbone Memorial Hospital in Surrey had become vacant she had needed little persuasion to apply. It was an excellent career move and Hawksford was only an hour's drive from Portchester.

She paused again and turned to look back at the

town. Through the trees to the west she could see glimpses of the large modern building of the Spencer Rathbone, so very different from the Victorian hospital that she had left behind, and she felt a little surge of excitment at the thought of starting there on the following Monday morning.

She had also been lucky in finding accommodation, answering an advertisement in a medical journal for a third person to join two other midwives from the same hospital sharing the top-floor flat of a large house overlooking the town.

The house, like so many others in this old part of the town, was of mellow red brick, its many sash-windows divided into Georgian squares, some enhanced with portions of brightly coloured stained glass.

As Nicole climbed the steep drive she looked up at the house, which appeared to be slumbering gently in the afternoon heat beneath its covering of red-leaved creeper, and decided that everything really did seem to be turning out rather well.

Then, as she put her key in the lock, she pulled a little face—it had always been a fault of hers to count her chickens before they were hatched, and it was very early days yet to know whether her new life was going to be all she hoped. For a start, she had to meet her colleagues.

If, however, they all turned out to be like her two flat-mates, Mai-Lee Chang and Judith Taylor, life would be just perfect, but Nicole knew from past experience that that would be too much to hope for.

As the door swung open, her thoughts briefly returned to the incident in the bookshop. Normally she was irritated by any form of pick-up, but she was sure this hadn't been that.

It had been quite strange, she reflected, because for one moment she really had thought she'd met the man before and he had obviously thought the same thing. Maybe they had—although she felt certain, if that was the case, she would have remembered.

It wasn't, after all, every day that she met such a man: tall, of muscular build, with an air of authority about him, yet with amusement lurking in his dark eyes. . . No, she would have been sure to remember. . .

She began to climb the stairs. What was it he had said? She must have a twin? She smiled to herself as she reached the first landing and paused for one moment to look out of the window at the town far below.

Again, it was as if he'd known.

On the following Monday morning Nicole arrived at the Spencer Rathbone, parked her car in the staff car park and took the lift to the obstetric unit on the fourth floor.

As she walked to the nurses' station down a wide, carpeted corridor with its pastel-painted walls and framed abstract prints, Nicole was reminded more of a luxury hotel than a maternity hospital.

There were several nurses in the station and they looked up as Nicole approached. Before she had time even to introduce herself, however, the door of Sister's office opened and Judith Taylor, one of the women who shared her flat, appeared.

'Ah, Nicole.' Judith's face broke into a smile as

she caught sight of her. 'Welcome to Matty—this is Nicole, everyone.' Judith glanced round at the other girls. 'She's joining us as a staff midwife.'

There was a general chorus of hellos from the other staff, then Judith said, 'Come through and I'll show you your locker, then when you've changed into your uniform, I'll take you over the unit.'

Nicole had only seen Judith a couple of times at the flat but liked her already. She was a round-faced, softly spoken woman in her thirties, with a west-country accent and unruly dark hair that curled crisply round her ears.

In the locker-room Nicole changed quickly into her blue uniform, fastening the belt with the silver buckle her mother had given her when she qualified. Then, taking a comb from her handbag, she glanced round the room and moved across to a mirror on the far wall. She had recently had her hair cut and, although at first she'd had reservations, especially when the hairdresser had gathered up the long dark strands and held them up for her to see, now she was pleased. Her new short, smooth bob framed her oval face and the style, washed each morning under the shower and blow-dried into place, was so easy to maintain.

She paused for a moment before moving away from the mirror, staring at her reflection. Large, expressive brown eyes set in an olive complexion gazed back at her from above a short straight nose, a wide generous mouth and a chin which her mother called stubborn, but which Nicole preferred to think of as determined.

'Right, Dennington,' she said aloud to her reflection, 'get out there and show them what you're made of.' She grinned then—the smile transforming her serious expression—straightened her shoulders, smoothed down her uniform and, with one last glance to reassure herself that she looked presentable, crossed to the door and tugged it open.

Judith looked up from her desk as Nicole tapped on her door and pushed it open. 'Are you ready?' she smiled. 'Good, I'll show you round.'

'You'll spend most of your time here on Antenatal and the labour suites,' said Judith, as they left the nurses' station and began to walk down the wide corridor.

Open doors on either side offered glimpses of light, pleasant, four-bedded wards where heavily pregnant women with resigned, bored expressions, in dressing-gowns and slippers, shuffled up and down or rested, and from which snatches of conversations, laughter, music from radios, and the hustle and bustle of early-morning ward routine spilled out into the corridor.

Further on they passed the labour suites and delivery-rooms. From behind one door they heard the thin, unmistakable wail of a new-born baby.

'It's so large and airy compared with my last hospital,' said Nicole, as Judith opened doors to allow her to see storerooms and offices.

'A bit antiquated was it?' asked Judith with a chuckle.

'You could say that—oh, we coped, don't get me wrong, but this is so much more inspiring, somehow.' Nicole stopped and looked around. 'So where is Postnatal, for heaven's sake?'

'We haven't come to that yet,' Judith smiled. 'That's through here.' She pushed open a set of double doors which revealed yet more corridors and more suites of wards, most with four, some with six, beds.

Here the picture was different: the rooms were filled with flowers and cards congratulating the new mothers, while the patients themselves, though tired, were for the most part, unmistakably happy.

Some had their babies with them, were feeding or changing nappies, most looked up proudly as Judith and Nicole appeared, all eager to show off.

They moved on down the corridor, and the steadily growing volume of noise left no doubt as to which section they were now approaching.

'Welcome to the nursery suite.' Judith grinned, and they both stopped and looked around. Many small rooms opened out from one central station, all decorated in soft colours: lemon, peach and pale greens with friezes and curtains depicting a variety of nursery-rhyme characters. Each room had its own radiator, nursing chair, oxygen cylinders and resuscitation equipment, together with two or three tiny cots, the occupants wrapped in white cellular shawls, some sleeping, others loudly demanding attention.

'I love it here,' said Judith simply. 'It's what the whole thing is about.'

Nicole nodded. 'I know what you mean, but for me the greatest satisfaction is back there in the delivery-room and the look in a mother's eyes when you first hand her her new-born baby.'

'I know,' Judith nodded, 'I love that too.'

They moved on, then Judith said, 'There's something else I want you to see—come on, through here.' She pushed open yet more doors and they entered another area.

Here the atmosphere was different: quiet yet somehow highly charged, the much larger rooms packed with technical equipment.

'It's not really our department,' said Judith, her voice taking on a hushed tone in keeping with the surroundings, 'but here at the Spencer Rathbone everyone is intensely proud of the special care baby unit.'

'From what I've heard, you have every reason to be.' Nicole paused and looked round at the tiny, pre-term babies, some with a mass of tubes connecting them to monitors and other equipment, others wrapped in insulating material to prevent hypothermia, and at the staff, most gowned and masked, who moved silently around performing their everyday tasks so essential to the survival of these special, tiny patients.

'There's Mai-Lee.' Judith nodded towards a figure who had just entered the room by a door on the far side.

'I didn't realise she worked in SCBU.' Nicole smiled at the almond-shaped eyes that sparkled at them over a white mask.

'It's her whole life,' replied Judith simply.

They stayed a while, watching, and as a tall, grey-haired man joined Mai-Lee and began examining a baby wired to a heart monitor, Judith leaned towards Nicole and whispered, 'That's Edward Bridgeman, our consultant paediatrician.'

'I've heard of him,' Nicole whispered back, then, as Judith turned and she followed her from the ward, she added, 'He's a very eminent man.'

'Yes,' Judith agreed, speaking normally now as they re-entered the corridor, 'he is. We are very fortunate to have him here. In fact, we are fortunate all round where our team is concerned. Our consultant obstetrician is Matthew Fletcher—have you heard of him?'

'I'm not sure.' Nicole frowned, then shot Judith a glance. 'Should I have done?'

'Probably not. I just wondered, that's all—he writes in some of the medical journals.'

'Ah. . . I must admit the name did seem to ring a bell when you mentioned it,' said Nicole, as they began to walk back down the corridor.

'Well, you'll meet him later. He's doing his antenatal clinic and I was going to suggest you start off in there—that OK with you?'

'Yes, of course.' Nicole paused. 'Where is the clinic held, by the way?'

'In Outpatients—on the far side of the antenatal wards.' Judith grinned, 'well away from the labour suites.' She paused and threw Nicole a quick glance. 'You don't mind doing the clinic?'

'Of course not,' Nicole replied. 'Why should I?'

By this time they had returned to the nurses' station.

'It isn't everyone who likes the clinic.' As she spoke, Judith glanced at the fob-watch on the front of her uniform.

'Oh, I don't mind,' Nicole replied. Glancing round what was to become her new work-base, she noted with approval the healthy plants on the desk and windowsills, the colourful prints on the wall and the mass of picture postcards pinned to a cork notice-board. 'In fact,' she went on, 'I particularly like meeting the mums right at the beginning of their pregnancy, then seeing them at least a couple more times before their babies are born.'

'So do I,' agreed Judith. 'I think it's essential to establish some sort of relationship before that all-important encounter on the delivery-couch.' She paused. 'I'll take you over there now and introduce you to Ann, the receptionist. She's been there since the unit opened, and before that she was at the Royal Hawksford Infirmary.'

The clinic, as Judith had said, was well away from the labour suites, in one corner of the obstetric wing alongside the lifts. Apart from the usual Reception and offices, there was a large waiting area lined with comfortable seating, its walls covered with posters and information charts on everything from breast feeding to postnatal depression, from maternity benefits to pre-school playgroups. Another short corridor presumably led to the examination-rooms.

Ann Jennings greeted Nicole warmly and, after Judith had left to return to her own office, she poured coffee for them both from a cafetière along-side her desk.

'How many staff do you have in this clinic?' asked Nicole glancing round the pleasant waiting area and noting the play corner with its selection of toys, the vending-machine offering a choice of hot or cold drinks, and the large selection of magazines in neat piles on the low tables.

'We have three clerical staff on duty at any one time,' explained Ann. 'On the nursing side, for this antenatal clinic, there will be two midwives and two care assistants, a consultant obstetrician or registrar or, if he isn't available, a senior house officer.'

'I understand it's Mr Fletcher today,' said Nicole, sipping her coffee.

'Yes,' agreed Ann, 'it is. He's in his consulting-room at the moment dictating letters.' She paused. 'Have you met him yet?'

Nicole shook her head. 'No, not yet.'

'I'll take you down in a moment and introduce you,' said Ann briskly. 'There's nothing worse to my mind than having to meet one's new boss for the first time under the interested gaze of a patient.'

Ann's attention was taken then, by patients who were beginning to arrive in the lift, by the ringing of the telephone, and queries from her own staff.

Nicole found herself left to her own devices. Finishing her coffee, she wandered out of the reception area and made her way down the corridor to the examination-rooms. There was no sign of her fellow-midwife who would be assisting her in the clinic.

The first room she came to was the ultrasound unit with its array of modern technological equipment, used to perform scans on an unborn foetus in order to detect any problems.

The next room appeared to be some sort of office and, from the leaflets and literature on the desk, Nicole guessed it was the booking-room where new patients gave their details and booked beds for their confinements.

She was looking through some of the leaflets when she heard the sound of heavy footsteps and whistling outside in the corridor. She glanced up just as a figure in the familiar navy-blue uniform of the hospital porters appeared in the doorway.

The young man, his fair hair cut very short, stopped whistling when he was Nicole.

'Well, hello there!' His eyes lit up, then he grinned and looked round the office. 'Liz not here?'

'Er. . .no. . . I don't think so. . .' Nicole began uncertainly, but before she could enquire further as to who exactly Liz was, the porter stepped forward and placed a large envelope in her hands.

'Never mind, you'll do,' he said, nodding at her uniform. 'Can you see Mr Fletcher gets that immediately?'

'Oh, but——'

'I was told he wants this before the clinic starts.'

'Very well,' she nodded. 'I'll see he gets it.'

'Thanks.' The young man turned to go, then stopped and looked curiously at her. 'I haven't seen you here before, have I? His accent was cockney.

'No.' She shook her head. 'I'm new, it's my first day.'

'Nice to have you aboard.' He grinned again, his smile showing his approval. 'Dave Burns—general dogsbody.'

'Hello, Dave—Nicole Dennington.'

'See you around, Nicole.' With a wave of his hand he was gone. Seconds later she heard him whistling again, picking up the tune where he had left off.

She looked down at the envelope in her hands, then walked to the door and looked out into the corridor. There was no one around, but the growing noise from the reception area suggested the staff there were all busy.

She glanced round at the closed doors of the examination-rooms, then saw that one at the far end of the corridor had a plaque on it.

Slowly she walked towards it and on closer inspection could see that it read, 'Matthew Fletcher. Consultant Obstetrician'.

She hesitated only a moment longer, staring down at the envelope, then with a shrug she squared her shoulders and knocked on the door.

A deep, male voice bade her enter. She turned the handle and pushed the door open.

Her first impression was of a large room with sunlight flooding through the picture window which looked out across Hawksford to the distant hills.

A man was standing in front of the window, his back to the door. He was wearing a white coat and his hair was dark, but with the bright light behind him that was all that Nicole could discern.

A woman seated to one side of the large oak desk looked up sharply from her notebook. She looked to Nicole to be in her thirties, with vibrant red hair that tumbled over her shoulders. She narrowed her eyes—green eyes, Nicole noticed—set in a heart-shaped face, her complexion very pale like so many redheads'.

'What is it?' She stared indignantly at Nicole as if challenging her effrontery in disturbing the consultant.

'I was asked to see that Mr Fletcher gets this before clinic starts,' replied Nicole.

'It could have waited——' began the redhead.

'What is it, Louise?' The man spoke without turning. 'Is there a problem?'

Nicole looked up sharply. She knew that voice—deep, slightly husky—she'd heard it before. Heard it only recently. . .but—but it couldn't be. Surely not. It was impossible.

But even before he finally turned to face her, she knew it was.

Mr Matthew Fletcher, the senior consultant obstetrician of the Spencer Rathbone Memorial Hospital was the man she'd met the previous Saturday afternoon in the bookshop in town. The man she thought she'd met before, the man who thought he too had previously met her.

CHAPTER TWO

AGAIN the recognition flared in their eyes and for one moment, a moment that seemed suspended in time, it was as if they were alone in the room, as if the red-haired secretary had ceased to exist.

'Well, hello.' It was Matthew Fletcher who apparently recovered first. 'We meet again.'

'Yes.' Nicole continued to stare at him as if she were caught in some sort of trance, unable to believe that he was head of the obstetrics team that she was now a part of.

'Quite a coincidence,' he murmured, moving forward, away from the bright light in the window, so that Nicole could now see his face clearly. The same strong features, the dark eyes with the gleam of amusement in their depths, the dark hair with the few flecks of grey. . .

It was the sudden sound of the secretary noisily clearing her throat that jerked Nicole back to the present. She looked down at the woman and saw that she was looking from one to the other of them with barely concealed exasperation, as if she was wondering what on earth was going on.

Matthew Fletcher must have realised at the same moment for he too cleared his throat.

'I'm sorry, Louise.' He appeared to tear his gaze away from Nicole. 'It's just that I met this lady in town—we both thought we'd met before. . . It was a surprise seeing her here. . .'

The secretary's sceptical look left Nicole in no doubt what she was thinking.

Matthew Fletcher, however, appeared oblivious and allowed his gaze to move swiftly back to Nicole. 'I don't even know your name. . .' He trailed off, his gaze travelling over her uniform.

'Nicole.' She knew she sounded breathless and wished she didn't. 'Nicole Dennington,' she added in a concentrated attempt to pull herself together.

'Matthew Fletcher.' He held out his hand and after only a second's hesitation she stepped forward and took it. His fingers were cool and strong, the handshake firm, his hand entirely enclosing her much smaller one.

Some handshakes were barely more than the fleeting touch of fingers. Matthew Fletcher's wasn't like that: his was decisive, a positive manoeuvre.

She suddenly realised he was waiting, without releasing her hand, waiting as if he expected her to volunteer some sort of explanation.

'I—I've just joined the team,' she stammered, furious to feel her cheeks begin to colour, beneath not only Matthew Fletcher's gaze, but also that of his flame-haired secretary.

'As a permanent member of staff?' He raised his eyebrows.

'Yes,' she nodded.

'Ah.' He smiled, and in the silence that followed Nicole was vaguely aware of the sound of a klaxon as an ambulance hurtled towards the hospital. 'I thought,' he said at last, 'you might have been a temp.'

She shook her head and only then did he release her hand and move back behind his desk. 'Welcome to Spencer Rathbone and to the team,' he said, then added, 'This is Louise Collard, my personal secretary.'

The red-haired woman only barely inclined her head, acknowledging the introduction, then she returned her attention to her notepad.

'I understand you have something for me.' He spoke again and Nicole blinked.

He nodded towards the envelope in her hands and she looked down at it. For one moment she'd quite forgotten why she had come into the room in the first place.

'Oh, yes, yes, of course.' Flustered now by the whole episode, she took a deep breath and handed him the envelope. 'A porter gave it to me,' she said, 'and asked if I would make sure that you received it before the clinic started.'

'Thank you.' As he took the envelope his gaze met hers and yet again she detected that gleam of amusement in his eyes. Hastily she averted her own gaze. What in the world was the matter with her? She was behaving like a silly schoolgirl. It was out of character for Nicole to act like that and suddenly she felt irritated with herself for having let her confusion show, especially in front of the secretary. She turned away and stepped towards the door.

But Matthew Fletcher hadn't finished with her.

'Are you on duty in the clinic this morning or are you going back to the wards?' he asked.

She stopped, and without turning said, 'I'm not going back to the wards. Sister Taylor asked me to assist with clinic.'

'Good,' he replied lightly. 'I'll join you in a few minutes.'

She fled then, out of the room, down the short corridor to the booking-room where she hoped she could spend a few minutes recovering in private and cool her burning cheeks.

It was not to be, however, for as she pushed open the door of the office a young woman with straight blonde hair, finely chiselled features and wearing the uniform of a staff nurse, looked up from the desk.

'Oh, I'm sorry,' gasped Nicole, 'I didn't think there was anyone in here.'

'That's OK—come on in.' The woman smiled. 'You must be Nicole Dennington, Judith told me to expect you, I'm Liz Buchanan.' She frowned suddenly, her eyes narrowing. 'I say, are you all right? You look a bit hot and bothered.'

'No, it's OK, I'm fine.' Nicole attempted a smile and smoothed her hair into place.

'Where were you?' Liz raised her eyebrows and began sorting through some papers on the desk.

'What do you mean?' Nicole frowned.

'When I came in, they said in Reception that you had arrived, but I couldn't find you. I thought perhaps you'd heard rumours about how monstrous we are here on clinic, had second thoughts and hightailed it back to the labour suites.'

'Oh, no.' Nicole relaxed. 'No, nothing like that.' She shook her head. 'In fact I quite like outpatient clinics.'

'So where were you?'

'I was in Mr Fletcher's office.' As she said it she knew the colour touched her cheeks again, just as she knew the other girl saw it.

'Were you now?' Liz Buchanan raised one eyebrow. 'And what, may I ask, were you doing in with

the great man himself in your first few minutes on
the unit?'

'I. . . A porter asked me to give him an envelope. . .that's all.' Casually Nicole tried to defend
her actions.

'I see.' Liz gave a little shrug and looked down at
the desk again.

Nicole gave an inward sigh of relief. She was still
uncertain what exactly had happened to her and just
why she had reacted in the way she had to Matthew
Fletcher. All she did know was that she wanted to
forget the whole thing—at least for the time being.
Later, when she had the time, she might try to
analyse it, but for the moment she simply wanted to
get on with her work.

She waited, fully expecting Liz to tell her what she
wanted her to do. Instead the other girl began toying
with a set of folders and when at last she did speak
again it had nothing to do with their work schedule
for that morning.

'So what did you think of him?' she asked, throwing Nicole a sidelong glance from beneath her
eyelashes.

'Who?' Nicole's heart sank, knowing full well
what she meant, but playing for time, afraid of
showing how much her encounter with the consultant had thrown her.

'Who?' Liz eyed her up and down. 'Matthew
Fletcher, of course.' There was a touch of amused
exasperation in her voice.

'What do you mean, what did I think of him? I've
only just met him—I was only in him room for a few
minutes.'

'That's usually long enough.' Liz grinned.

'I don't understand.' Nicole frowned, uncomfortable now with the whole thing but with a growing sense of curiosity as to what the other girl meant.

'It's quite simple. A few minutes is usually long enough for most women to succumb to Matthew Fletcher's charm.'

Nicole shrugged, in a desperate attempt to appear nonchalant.

'Don't tell me you were oblivious to it——' Liz stared at her '—because I won't believe you,' she added, than laughed, and there was something so infectious about her laughter that Nicole found herself joining in. 'Go on, admit it, he's attractive, more attractive than the average consultant. . . Think about it, have you worked with one more attractive than him?'

'No,' Nicole agreed reluctantly, 'if you put it like that, I don't suppose I have. Yes, you're right, he is attractive,' she admitted at last.

'The thing is,' sighed Liz, 'he's nice with it. So nice that if you're not careful you end up thinking you're special. . .but he's like it to everyone. . .' She trailed off, then frowned. 'Was the Red Dragon with him?'

'The Red Dragon?' Nicole looked up, startled.

'Yes, his secretary, Louise?'

'Oh, yes.' She smiled then. 'Yes, she was.'

'It's her last week here.'

'Really?'

'Yes, she's moving to another job in London. Can't say I'm sorry. I've never been keen on her.' Liz glanced at her fob-watch as she spoke and give a little shriek. 'Oh my goodness, is that the time? We must get a move on. If there's one thing Mr Fletcher can't stand, it's unpunctuality. He expects that first patient to be ready for him on the dot. Come on, let's go through the list.'

The first two patients of the morning were a young woman, Mandy Jones, in the nineteenth week of her pregnancy, who had been suffering problems with high blood-presssure, and Sharon Richards, a girl of fifteen, on her first visit to the unit, who was accompanied by her mother.

'Nicole, would you like to take Sharon to the booking-room?' asked Liz, picking up the folder on Mandy Jones. 'Mr Fletcher will want to see Sharon as it's her first visit—I'll get him to see Mandy first, then when you've finished taking Sharon's particulars, I'll get him to come along to see her.'

Nicole hurried back to the waiting area, which had filled up alarmingly, and above the hubbub of voices she called Sharon Richard's name.

The girl, her long, permed hair dyed blonde, looked very young. Her mother, a thin, anxious woman, kept looking at her watch.

Together they followed Nicole to the booking-room and after she'd shut the door they sat down on the two chairs she indicated.

'Hello, Sharon, Mrs Richards.' Nicole smiled from the girl to her mother. 'My name is Nicole Dennington—I'm a midwife and I'd just like to take some details so that we can book a bed for Sharon for when her baby is born.'

Sharon was staring at the floor and didn't look up.

Her mother looked at her watch again. 'Will it take long?' she asked then, not waiting for Nicole to reply, she went on, 'Only I've got to get to work. I daren't be late—they're laying people off left, right and centre—I can't risk losing this job—not with my Dennis out of work.'

'Your husband's unemployed?' Nicole looked up from Sharon's record folder which she'd opened and placed on the desk.

Mrs Richards nodded. 'Yes, has been for two years—no pospect of getting anything else either.'

'So where do you work, Mrs Richards?'

'Biscuit factory.'

Nicole nodded. Already she knew that the well-known biscuit manufacturer who had large premises just outside Hawksford provided a lot of employment in the town.

'We'll try to keep things as brief as we can,' she said, not unsympathetically, for while she felt for Sharon, she also knew the anguish so many people were suffering from unemployment.

'Now, Sharon.' She turned her attention to the girl, who was still silent and staring at the ground. 'I see from your records that you have already seen the hospital social worker and that you are twenty weeks pregnant?'

'Yes, that right, Nurse.' Predictably, it was the girl's mother who answered for her.

'Your estimated date of delivery is the twenty-seventh of November, so we'll book you in around that time.' Rapidly Nicole began to fill in the relevant details on the forms, asking questions about Sharon's previous medical history and that of her family. When she came to the section dealing with the patient's occupation, she paused. 'I see your social worker reports you are still attending school,' she said at last.

Again, although Nicole directed the question at Sharon, it was her mother who answered.

'Yes, she's still at school. Mr Simmonds—her headmaster—he's been very good about it. Well, let's face it,' Mrs Richards sniffed, 'she isn't the first, is she? Not by a long chalk, she isn't especially at that school, and she won't be the last either, you mark my words.'

'Are you enjoying being at school, Sharon?' Nicole persisted.

'You like school, don't you, Sharon?' Her mother turned sharply and looked at her daughter.

'I used to like it,' the girl said, speaking for the first time.

'But not so much now?' asked Nicole quietly.

At that, Sharon at last looked up and met Nicole's glance. 'No.' She shook her head. 'Not so much now.'

'But I thought you liked school. . .' Her mother looked bewildered.

'Maybe it's a bit difficult just at the present—' began Nicole.

'I don't see why,' said Mrs Richards indignantly, 'Like I said, it's not as if she's the first. . .'

'Sharon,' Nicole went on gently, 'the doctor will want to examine you in a few minutes' time. Would you like to go over there into the changing-room and get undressed? Put on the white gown that opens down the back, then slip on the robe that is hanging behind the door.'

Sharon stood up and for one moment Nicole detected fear in her eyes. 'It's all right,' she began, but was cut short by Mrs Richards, who also stood up.

'Would anyone mind if I went now? You'll be all right, won't you, Sharon?'

Again, in the second before the girl lowered her gaze, Nicole detected fear in her eyes.

'I think you should stay while Sharon has her examination, Mrs Richards,' said Nicole firmly. 'I'm sure Mr Fletcher would like you to be there —and I daresay Sharon would as well.'

The girl gave a nonchalant shrug as if it was of little consequence to her what her mother did, but Nicole suspected that underneath her apparent air of bravado she was relieved.

'Who is this doctor?' asked Mrs Richards, while Sharon was undressing.

'Mr Fletcher,' replied Nicole. 'He's the consultant obstetrician.'

The woman frowned. 'You mean he's a specialist?'

'Yes, that's right.'

'There's nothing wrong with Sharon, is there?'

'Not that I'm aware of. . .'

'So why's she seeing a specialist?'

'It's purely routine, Mrs Richards,' Nicole explained. 'Sharon is very young and Mr Fletcher will want to check that all is going well with her pregnancy.'

The woman was silent for a long moment, then she sighed. 'No chance I could have a cigarette, I suppose?' she said at last.

Nicole smiled and shook her head. 'I'm sorry, no. Not in here.' She glanced down at the social worker's notes in front of her. 'I see that Sharon smokes, Mrs Richards—it would be much better for her and for the baby if she was to give it up, at least during her pregnancy, if not permanently.'

'Yes, I know. . .it's hard though. We've all been through it just lately.'

'Yes, I can imagine.' Nicole nodded.

'God only knows what's going to happen afterwards. . .' Mrs Richards sighed again, as if the subject had been a bone of contention in her household.

'The baby's father. . .?' Nicole began hesitantly.

'No-good young tearaway—will end up inside, the rate he's going. . .' Mrs Richards trailed off as the door of the changing-room opened and Sharon reappeared. She threw her mother a contemptuous glance as if she guessed what she had been talking about.

Further conversation was prevented as there came a knock on the outer door. Nicole called out, the door opened and Liz popped her head round.

'Are you ready for Mr Fletcher?' she asked.

'Yes.' Nicole nodded and stood up. 'Come on, Sharon,' she said kindly, 'and you, Mrs Richards, come with me.'

They all followed Liz down the corridor and she showed them into one of the examination-rooms. As Liz disappeared outside, Nicole indicated for Mrs Richards to take a seat in the corner of the room, then she helped Sharon on to the examination-couch.

Only moments later there came a brief knock, the door was opened and Matthew Fletcher strode into the room.

Carefully, Nicole avoided his gaze.

'Hello, Sharon.' He smiled down at her and the

girl gazed up at him, the fear only too apparent now in her eyes. 'What did you reckon to EastEnders last night?' he asked.

'I—I. . .' Sharon began to stutter, but before she could form an answer he went on. 'I think that young woman is making a big mistake—she'll live to regret it, don't you think?'

'Well, yes, I suppose she will,' agreed a startled Sharon.

'Mind you,' Matthew Fletcher went on, 'I said all that would happen, right at the start. I said that was going to happen. . .did you think so too?'

'Yes, I did,' Sharon agreed, her gaze flickering for a moment to her mother who was looking equally uncertain.

During the next five minutes, as they continued to discuss the recent goings-on in Albert Square, Matthew Fletcher carried out his examination.

When he had finished, he smiled down at Sharon. 'I'll be taking care of you, Sharon, right up until the time your baby is born,' he said, 'Oh, I daresay I'll have a little help from my friends——' he looked up suddenly and his gaze met Nicole's '—but most of the time, it'll be you and me. So we'll see if we're right about what happens in EastEnders—they should have battled it all out by November—don't you think?'

Sharon nodded, then suddenly, unexpectedly, she smiled. It was the first time Nicole had seen her smile and it transformed her features, lighting up the sullen little face, and it had been Matthew Fletcher who was responsible.

He lingered for a moment, unhurried, talking to Sharon, and Nicole found herself studying him, wondering what it was about him that had made such an impact on her.

He was attractive, it was true, in a darkly masculine sort of way, but it was more than that, much more than that. He had made her feel special, made her feel she was the only person who mattered.

But what was it Liz had said? He was like that with everyone?

She shifted from one foot to the other. Hadn't he just proved it with Sharon and the way he had handled her situation? But what if he had? Did it matter? Did it matter to her, Nicole?

Of course it didn't, she told herself firmly. It was nothing whatsoever to do with her how Matthew Fletcher behaved towards other people—she really was being quite ridiculous where he was concerned. After all, she barely knew the man, had only met him twice: that one meeting in the bookshop and today at the hospital.

True, that bookshop meeting had been strange, to say the least——

'Is that all right, Staff Nurse?'

She jumped, shaken out of her daydreams, and realised Matthew Fletcher had been speaking to her and she hadn't heard a word he'd been saying.

'I'm sorry,' she mumbled, glancing from him to Sharon, then to Mrs Richards who was looking at her watch again. 'What did you say?'

'You were miles away.' The amusement was back in his eyes and Nicole felt herself squirm in embarrassment. 'I merely said to Sharon that you would carry on with her tests: weight, urine, blood-pressure, et cetera.'

'Oh, yes, of course.' To hide her confusion Nicole

began to bustle about the small room, fiddling with instruments and paper sheeting.

'Is it all right if I go now?' asked Mrs Richards suddenly, a note of desperation in her voice.

Matthew Fletcher turned to look at her in surprise.

'Mrs Richards has to get to work,' explained Nicole quickly.

'Then of course you must go.' He smiled at her. 'You can leave Sharon safely in the hands of Staff Midwife Dennington.'

'Oh.' The woman looked bewildered at first, as if it was totally alien to her to be treated with such courtesy. 'Oh, right, well, thank you.' She smiled then and added, 'I'll see you later, Sharon.'

The girl nodded and her mother sidled uncertainly from the room. Matthew Fletcher prepared to follow her, then paused in the doorway and looked back.

'See you soon, Sharon.' He grinned. 'Don't forget to take your iron pills, will you? Oh, and cut out the smoking.'

'All right.' She pulled a face, then grinned as he winked at her before leaving the room.

Nicole took a deep breath. 'Well, Sharon, it looks like it's you and me,' she said.

The girl nodded, remaining silent as Nicole set up the sphygmomanometer to check her blood-pressure. Then, as Nicole was securing the cuff on her upper arm, she suddenly spoke. 'He's nice, isn't he?'

Nicole nodded. 'Yes, very nice,' she agreed.

'He's not like a doctor.'

'Oh, I don't know.' Nicole began to pump the bulb, carefully noting the reading. 'There are plenty of nice doctors.'

'Not that nice.'

Sharon fell silent again, watching as Nicole noted the second reading and entered the result in her records.

'Now, Sharon, if you could just slip off the couch and on to the scales so that I can check your weight.' Nicole turned to the scales and began to adjust the weights.

When Sharon made no attempt to get down from the couch, she glanced up.

'Will he be there?'

Nicole frowned. The girl was still sitting on the edge of the couch swinging her legs. She looked very young, like a child herself. 'Will who be there, Sharon?' she asked gently.

'Him. Mr Fletcher—when it's born.'

'Oh, I see. Well, he may be, if he happens to be on duty at that time.'

'I hope he is.' She was silent again for a moment, then throwing Nicole a sidelong glance, she said, 'I'm not keeping it—the baby.'

'Really? When did you decide?'

'When the social worker came to the house I told her, and me mum, that I want it adopted.'

'What did your mum say, Sharon?'

'She didn't seem too keen—about it being adopted—but it's not up to her, is it? It's my baby and it's my life.'

'And it's what you want?'

'Yes.' Her reply was defiant, the look in her eyes hostile as she stared at Nicole, but as Nicole, calm and unmoved, gazed steadily back, the girl's stare became uncertain and in the end she lowered her eyes. 'I don't know,' she muttered. 'I think so.'

There was silence in the small room, broken only by the murmur of voices from the reception area. Then Sharon looked up again and briefly her gaze met Nicole's—the hopelessness only too apparent in the pale blue eyes. She shrugged. 'I don't know,' she said again.

'When do you officially leave school, Sharon?'

'Not till next summer when I'm sixteen.'

'And what do you want to do?'

'I was going to train to be a hairdresser. Now——' she shrugged again, the gesture summing up the hopelessness of her situation '—goodness knows.'

'What do your family think?'

'Oh, them!' Sharon gave an angry, helpless gesture.

'Your mum. . .?'

'Oh, mum was all right about it, I suppose, but I don't think she really understands. Dad was angry—kept going on about another mouth to feed—anyone would think I meant to get pregnant to hear him go on.'

'And didn't you?' Nicole asked quietly.

'Of course I didn't!' She looked up sharply, indignantly. 'I was on the pill, wasn't I?'

'You mean the pill failed? That's very rare, Sharon.'

The girl shrugged again and looked away. 'Maybe I forgot to take a few—I don't know. Well, you can't think of everything—anyway, why should it all be down to me. . .?'

'Your boyfriend?'

'If I'd left it to him, I'd have been pregnant long ago. . . Anyway, Jason isn't me boyfried now.'

'Isn't he?'

'No. He cleared off as soon as he knew—scared, I suppose. . .'

'You are under age, Sharon.'

'Yeah, I know.'

'Listen.' Gently Nicole touched the girl's shoulder. 'If you want to talk at any time, you can always come and see me.'

'OK, thanks.' Her reply was brief, almost gruff, and moments later, after Nicole had finally checked her weight, she said, 'Is that all?'

Nicole nodded. 'Yes, I've checked your urine, that's all right, so you can get dressed now.'

Nicole, watching thoughtfully as Sharon sauntered back down the corridor to the changing-room, was joined by Liz, who stared after Sharon's retreating figure, then said. 'How did you get on with her?'

'All right, I think,' Nicole replied slowly, then added. 'Better after her mother had left—but it's all very sad, isn't it?'

Liz nodded. 'Yes, she never told anyone about her pregnancy, apparently, until she was over four months—and she's only one. We see far too many like Sharon.' She paused, then said, I suppose Mr Fletcher wreaked his usual charm on her.'

'He did,' Nicole admitted.

'He's especially good with the teenagers—he brings himself right to their level somehow, but whereas if some people did that it would sound patronising, with Matthew Fletcher you get the impression he really means it.'

'Not only with the teenagers,' remarked Nicole. 'I would hazard a guess that Sharon's mother fell victim to his charm as well.'

Liz laughed. 'That doesn't surprise me.' She

glanced down at the list in her hand. 'Well, this won't do,' she said, 'we must get on.'

'So who's next?'

'There's a Mrs Rose in room number four—she's to have an ultrasound scan today, then Mr Fletcher will want to see her.' Liz paused. 'She's expecting twins,' she added at last. 'Would you like to do the usual checks, Nicole?'

'Twins, you say?' Nicole looked up quickly.

'Yes,' Liz nodded. 'Does that interest you especially?'

'It most certainly does,' Nicole replied with a smile.

CHAPTER THREE

BRIDGET ROSE, a bright-faced Irish woman in her late twenties, was radiant with the full flush of her pregnancy.

While Nicole carried out the usual routine checks, Bridget chatted happily to her.

'How does your husband feel about having twins?' Nicole asked as she helped Bridget on to the couch ready for her examination.

'I think he's more apprehensive than I am.' Bridget laughed and pushed back her long dark hair. 'He really isn't sure what to expect.'

'Well, that's understandable,' replied Nicole.

'After all,' Bridget went on, 'it's twice the work they'll be, isn't it?'

'That's true,' Nicole agreed, 'but don't forget they'll also be twice the fun, and twice the joy,' she added.

'You sound as if you've had some experience of twins.' Bridget looked curiously at her.

'You could say that,' Nicole replied, 'but not in the way you mean. I've delivered twins and assisted at a couple of Caesarean births—but my knowledge of caring for twins as babies is more personal,' she smiled. 'Most of it comes from what my mother has told me.'

'Your mother?' Bridget Rose's eyes widened.

'Yes, I am a twin.' Nicole replied.

38

'Are you now?' Bridget's face lit up. 'Isn't that exciting?'

'Twins are special, Bridget, believe me.' Nicole went on. 'Not only special to their parents and those around them, but very special to each other.'

Bridget opened her mouth to ask more questions, but at that moment Liz came into the room accompanied by Matthew Fletcher, and her attention was diverted.

'Hello, Bridget and how are the three of you today?' The consultant smiled down at her.

'We are all well, Mr Fletcher, thank you.' Bridget beamed back. 'We've had our scan— have you seen it?'

'I have indeed,' he replied, 'and two healthier babies I couldn't wish to see. All I need to do now is to see that all is well with their mum.'

Bridget wriggled herself down on the couch and Nicole stepped forward to help her with her gown.

'Nurse was just telling me about how special twins are,' Bridget said a moment later, as the consultant began his examination.

'Was she indeed?' He answered without looking up.

'Well, she should know, shouldn't she?' Bridget carried on. 'Straight from the horse's mouth, so to speak.'

'What do you mean?' Still he didn't look up, continuing his examination of her abdomen.

Suddenly Nicole felt uncomfortable and wished she hadn't been quite so forthcoming about her personal details.

'Nurse is a twin herself. . .' Bridget rushed on, then she paused and frowned.

Matthew Fletcher looked up, his eyes meeting Nicole's across the couch.

'Is she now?' he said softly, the dark eyebrows rising in interested surprise.

'Didn't you know?' Bridget Rose looked from one to the other in obvious bewilderment. 'I thought you would have known. . .'

'Nurse Dennington has only just joined the team,' he replied quietly. 'I know very little about her. . . at the moment.'

Hastily Nicole looked away, aware that Liz, who was still in the room, had looked up in interest at the sudden turn of events.

'I hope you and Nurse Dennington will be able to deliver my twins,' Bridget chattered on, apparently unaware of the heightened interest in the room.

'I shall certainly make every effort to be present when the time comes,' replied Matthew Fletcher, 'and I'm sure Nurse Dennington will do her best, won't you, Nurse?'

'Of course.' Nicole smiled down at Bridget, then as the consultant moved away she proceeded to assist her to get up from the couch.

'I can't imagine how I can get any bigger—and I have another six weeks to go,' Bridget laughed. 'As it is, I can't get out of the bath on my own.'

'Maybe it would be easier to take showers at the moment,' suggested Nicole, then, as Bridget Rose trundled off to get dressed, she turned to Liz. 'Who's next?' she asked.

'So you're a twin?' Liz ignored her question.

'Yes,' Nicole nodded.

'Twins always fascinate me,' Liz said. 'And I'm not the only one. I should think you'd be quite a point of interest around here. . . Tell me, are you and your twin——?' She broke off in mid-sentence as someone outside in the corridor suddenly called her name. With a muttered exclamation, followed by a sigh, she hurried from the room, leaving Nicole wondering what it was she had been about to ask.

The rest of the morning seemed to pass in a flash as more patients were booked in, others received mid-pregnancy check-ups or scans, one was transferred to the ward as her labour had started and her blood-pressure was high, and another was admitted with a threatened miscarriage.

Before Nicole knew it the clinic was over, and she made her way to the large staff cafeteria on the third floor.

It was very crowded as it was lunchtime, but Nicole could not see anyone she knew so, after selecting lasagne and salad and a pot of tea, she took herself off to a seat beside the window where she could enjoy an uninterrupted view of the castle and the park.

The first day in any new job could be nerve-racking but Nicole was feeling quite satisfied with the way she had coped with the morning on Outpatients. Apart from the tension of her encounters with Matthew Fletcher, which she found she was totally at a loss to explain, she felt she had got off to a good start.

That Matthew Fletcher had had some sort of profound effect on her, she was reluctantly prepared to admit, but the nature of the effect was totally beyond her, as was the fact that their meeting had seemed to have a similar effect on him.

She had almost finished her lunch when out of the

corner of her eye she saw him come into the cafeteria. He was accompanied by his secretary and, as they chose their food, then looked round for a table, Nicole averted her gaze, swiftly looking out of the window. The last thing she wanted was to have Matthew Fletcher and his condescending secretary join her.

A moment later, however, she sensed someone beside her and, glancing up, saw to her dismay that it was him.

'So I was right,' he said, raising his eyebrows and smiling down at her.

'I beg your p—pardon?' she stammered, half expecting him to sit down beside her. When he remained standing she realised that his hands were empty and, looking beyond him, she saw his tray on the table next to hers where he must have put it before walking across to her. Louise meanwhile was unloading her own tray.

'I was right,' he repeated. 'When me met in town. . .when we thought we'd met before. When we agreed we hadn't, I said you must have a twin. . . I didn't for one moment imagine that you had, it was simply a figure of speech.'

'Oh, I see,' she replied, aware that Louise was glaring at her.

'Maybe it was your twin I met before,' he said, 'and that was the reason I thought I knew you.'

'I doubt it,' she replied.

He had started to move away to rejoin Louise and begin his lunch, which even now was cooling on the plate, but at Nicole's words he stopped, then came back, staring down at her again. 'I'm sorry——' there was a slight frown now between the dark eyebrows '—what did you say?'

'I said, I doubted it.'

'Doubted what?' He was really puzzled now.

'That the reason you thought you knew me was because you'd met my twin,' she explained quietly.

'Oh?' He frowned. 'Why is that?'

Nicole took a deep breath. 'Because my twin is six feet tall, a captain in the army. . .and he also has a moustache.'

He stared at her for a long moment, then he threw back his head and laughed. 'I see,' he said at last. 'Well, it couldn't have been that, then.'

'No,' she agreed solemnly, 'it couldn't have been.' Then she too found herself laughing.

'Maybe you have a double,' he said.

'Are you one of those people that thinks everyone has a twin or a double?'

'Not necessarily.' His eyes gleamed with amusement. 'I do sometimes wonder if everyone doesn't have a soul-mate and if that isn't instantly recognisable. . .but that's another thing altogether.'

She felt her cheeks begin to grow warm under his scrutiny as she realised he was going into dangerous waters again.

'What I do have, however——' he grew serious again '—is an interest in twins, their behaviour and their development.' He paused, appearing to hesitate, then, apparently oblivious to Louise's attempts to attract his attention, and as if coming to a rapid decision, he went on, 'In fact, I'm in the process of compiling information—case-histories, personal experiences, that sort of thing—for a book which I'm writing on that very subject. . . I wonder. . .'

He paused again, eyeing her speculatively. 'Could we perhaps have a chat sometime. . .?'

'Yes, of course——' she began.

'Matthew! Your food is going cold,' called Louise.

'Yes, all right,' he replied absentmindedly over his shoulder, then, turning eagerly back to Nicole, said, 'So you would be prepared to help?'

'Yes. . .'

'Good,' he said briefly, as if that decided the matter. 'I'll get back to you,' he added.

He went then back to his own table and his impatient companion.

Moments later, Nicole finished her meal, pushed her cup and saucer away and stood up.

Without another glance in Matthew Fletcher's direction, but at the same time fully aware that as she passed his table he was watching her, she hurried from the cafeteria and took the stairs to the fourth floor to report back to Judith.

'So how did it go?' Judith eyed her with interest.

'Pretty well—I think. It'll be better next time,' she added, 'now that I know Liz's routine.'

'You got on all right with Liz?'

'Oh, yes, she's nice.'

'And the others?'

'Yes, fine. . .' She swallowed, not trusting herself even to mention Matthew Fletcher, then, as Judith picked up her telephone receiver to make a call, she took a deep breath. What in the world was wrong with her? She really would have to pull herself together—she couldn't remember ever behaving like this before.

'Where would you like me now?' she asked, as Judith waited for the phone to be answered.

'You've only got another hour before the end of your shift,' Judith replied, glancing at her watch, 'so could you give me a hand with these reports?'

'Of course.' Nicole nodded, then, as Judith began talking into the receiver, she picked up the pile of folders from the desk.

She worked quietly and steadily for the next hour on the reports, while Judith continued with phone calls and arranging staff rotas, then suddenly, just as she was thinking it was time to be going home, right out of the blue, Judith casually said, 'How did you get on with Matthew Fletcher?'

She looked up sharply. Had Judith heard anything? But that was absurd: what could she have heard? There was nothing to hear, for heaven's sake.

'Oh, I thought he was very nice,' she mumbled.

'Most people do,' observed Judith drily. 'Had you met him before?'

'What do you mean?' Startled, she looked up and stared at Judith.

The sister frowned. 'Nothing. I just wondered if you'd come across him before, that's all, perhaps in another hospital or when you were training—you did say earlier that you thought his name rang a bell.'

'Oh, no,' she replied hurriedly, in relief, 'nothing like that.'

'I only wondered,' Judith shrugged. 'Have you finished those reports?'

'Yes.'

'In that case I think it's time you called it a day.'

'Are you going home as well?'

'Yes, just about. If you'd like to wait a few minutes, I'll be with you.'

They walked back to the flat together, through the park and out of the town, then up the hill through the narrow, cobbled streets.

'So you think you're going to like it at the Spencer Rathbone?' asked Judith, puffing slightly as they reached the top of the hill.

'Oh, yes,' replied Nicole, 'and if nothing else, it will keep me fit doing this climb every day.'

'I thought that,' remarked Judith ruefully. 'Trouble is, I also gave up smoking when I came here and have been over-compensating with sweets, hence this extra weight I've got to contend with.' She patted her stomach.

'Well, I've been feeling a bit unfit lately,' said Nicole. 'I used to ride regularly but got out of the habit when I was up in Stockport. I must get round to finding some riding-stables.'

'Oh, I believe there are several around Hawksford,' said Judith.

'I'll have to make some enquiries,' Nicole replied, 'that is, if this hill doesn't get the better of me first!'

Pausing for a moment, she looked up at the house, then with a little sigh she followed Judith inside and climbed the stairs.

She had been delighted when she had first seen the flat, with its beautiful views across the town. The rooms were spacious and airy, the women having their own bed-sitting-rooms and sharing the bathroom and kitchen.

Already, in the short time she had been there, Nicole had stamped her personality on her room adding cushions, duvet and curtains to the furnishings in her favourite beiges, russets and creams, and to the walls prints and posters, scenes of Tuscany and Provence.

On the dressing-table, beside photographs of her twin, Richard, and other members of her family, she had arranged the cut-glass scent-bottles that she had been collecting for several years, and on the oak shelves that almost covered one wall she had displayed her treasured books.

In the hearth, with its surround of bottle-green ceramic tiles, she had stood an earthenware jug filled with dried flowers and grasses.

Already she was beginning to love the flat, just as she had begun to love the old town and the prospect of working at the modern hospital.

So why was it that during that evening, after her first day at work, she felt restless, pacing the floor and unable to settle to anything?

In the end, she reluctantly admitted to herself that it was her encounters with Matthew Fletcher that were playing on her mind. She still couldn't come to terms with the impact he seemed to have had upon her, any more than she could accept the fact that since their meeting he seemed to be constantly on her mind. She knew she really would have to get a grip on herself—after all, she was going to be working in close proximity to him for some considerable time.

Already his flame-haired secretary had shown her annoyance at the rapport there seemed to be between the two of them.

She wondered about Louise. Maybe there was more to her relationship with the consultant then merely that of secretary and boss—she didn't know—but if there was, it should be of no concern to her. She really did have to get her emotions under control, she told herself firmly, as she finally prepared for bed that night.

But after she had switched off her bedside light, the last thought that entered her mind before falling asleep was that Liz had said that Louise was leaving soon.

And her first thought upon waking the following morning was that Matthew Fletcher had asked her to help him with his book.

She didn't, however, see much of the consultant obstetrician during the next few days, just glimpses as he attended a birth, or through the open doorway of his consulting-room. He was a very busy man and seemed to have little time for socialising or trivialities.

Nicole was reluctantly just beginning to think he had forgotten asking her to help him with his research when, late one morning, he was called to attend a patient who had suffered a haemorrhage following the birth of her baby.

After he had examined and reassured the young woman, he strode into the nurses' station.

'I would like Mrs White prepared for Theatre, please,' he said firmly. 'I will see her before this afternoon's list—she requires a D&C. Has the paediatrician seen baby White yet?'

'Yes.' It was Judith who answered. 'It looks as if all is well there.'

'Excellent,' he replied. 'All that remains, then, is for us to make the mother more comfortable.' He turned to walk away, then caught sight of Nicole, who had come into the station to change her apron, which had become soiled during the birth.

'Ah, Nurse Dennington,' he said. 'I've been meaning to have a word with you—could you come along to my consulting-room, please, before you go off duty?'

'Yes, of course, Mr Fletcher,' she replied. She threw a quick glance at Judith, and was relieved to see she had moved out of earshot. 'That will be about one o'clock.'

'That's fine—my theatre list doesn't start until two.'

He nodded and moved away and, to her dismay, Nicole found her pulse was racing. So much for trying to keep calm, she told herself ruefully.

She wasn't sure how she got through the rest of her shift and, to her disgust, she found her gaze continually straying to the clock.

By the time she knocked on Matthew Fletcher's door her nerves were stretched to breaking-point. As the door opened she turned eagerly, only to be disappointed to find Louise in the doorway.

'Is Mr Fletcher there?' He gaze slid past Louise to the room beyond.

'No, he isn't.' The reply was abrupt, almost rude.

'He asked me to meet him here at one o'clock,' said Nicole evenly, aware as she spoke of the slight narrowing of the woman's eyes.

'You'd better come in, then.' Reluctantly, she stood aside for Nicole to enter.

The room was indeed empty, and on the far side the door to another office, presumably Louise's stood open. Nicole caught a glimpse of stacks of books and papers, several pot-plants lined up on a desk, and an open hold-all on the floor, and she suddenly remembered hearing someone say that it was today the secretary was leaving.

'Where is your new job, Louise?' she asked, trying to be sociable.

The woman arched her eyebrows, and for one moment Nicole thought she was going to tell her to mind her own business, then she gave a slight shrug. 'Harley Street,' she replied. 'I've been offered a post as PA to a senior consultant in a private clinic.'

'That sounds marvellous,' said Nicole.

'It'll be better than this.' Louise glanced contemptuously round the room. 'Considerably more money, for a start. And, I would hope, a little more appreciation. You can slog your guts out, you know, for half a lifetime and at the end have nothing to show for it and get very little thanks into the bargain.'

From the bitter note in the other woman's voice, Nicole found herself wondering if Louise had been fired from her present position.

'You say he asked you to meet him here?' Louise had turned away towards her office, but she paused and looked curiously back at Nicole.

Nicole nodded. 'Yes, I'm to help him with some research.'

'Research? What sort of research?'

For one moment the role was reversed and Nicole was tempted to tell Louise to mind her own business. Instead, she swallowed and said evenly, 'For his book.'

'Why should he think you would be able to help with that?' Louise asked suspiciously.

'The fact that I happen to be a twin probably has

something to do with it,' replied Nicole, irritated now by the woman's attitude.

Louise stared at her for a long moment, then the ghost of a smile touched her lips and, in the silence that followed, Nicole felt decidedly uncomfortable.

'Well,' Louise said softly at last, 'that explains it——' She broke off abruptly, then, raising her eyebrows, she said, 'Care for a word of advice from one who knows?'

'What do you mean?' Nicole frowned.

'Just watch yourself where Matthew Fletcher is concerned, that's all.'

'Watch myself? I don't understand.'

Louise shrugged and, lifting her right had, studied her nails. Then, glancing at Nicole, she must have seen her puzzled frown. 'He'll use you,' she said bluntly.

Nicole took a deep breath. 'I can assure you I have no intention of allowing myself to be used by anyone.'

'I thought that. . .but I found out, as you no doubt will in time——'

'My relationship with Mr Fletcher is a professional one,' Nicole interrrupted sharply, 'and this meeting is purely to discuss his book. . .' She trailed off as the door suddenly opened and Matthew Fletcher himself appeared.

He paused in the open doorway and looked from one to the other of them as if he sensed the tension in the room.

'Oh, there you are,' said Louise. 'Nurse Dennington says she's come to assist you and is apparently raring to go, in spite of the fact that I've

been telling her what to expect. Anyway, I'll leave
you to it.' With an irritating smile hovering around
her lips, she walked across the room and into her
office, then shut the door firmly behind her.

CHAPTER FOUR

FOR one moment he stared at the closed door, his expression inscrutable, then he turned. 'Please, Nicole,' he said, 'sit down. You don't mind if I call you Nicole?'

She shook her head and sat down in the chair he indicated. She still felt bemused by Louise's warning, for surely that was what it had been when she had said that he would use her.

But how could he use her? She was only going to help him with some research, for heaven's sake, and very little harm could come to her here in his consulting-room in the heart of the busy obstetrics wing of the Spencer Rathbone.

'I want to hear everything about you.' He broke into her thoughts and, looking up sharply. Nicole found that he had sat down behind his desk and was leaning back in his leather chair. Toying with a propelling-pencil and with his head tilted to one side, he critically surveyed her through half-closed eyes.

He was still wearing his white coat. Unbuttoned down the front, it revealed a crisp, white shirt, patterned tie and pin-striped trousers. A stethoscope protruded from the top pocket of his coat, and as he twirled the pencil Nicole caught the gleam of gold cufflinks.

'Everything?' she echoed weakly, playing for

time, wishing her pulses weren't racing quite so fast, wishing he wasn't quite so attractive.

He laughed, revealing strong, very white teeth. 'Well, practically everything—certainly as much as you can remember from your childhood, your upbringing with your brother and your subsequent relationship with him.'

'I hardly know where to begin. . .'

'How about at the beginning?' The amusement was back in those dark eyes but, not giving Nicole time to feel foolish, he went on rapidly, 'For a start, where were you born?'

'In Sussex, but when we were a year old the family moved to Portchester in Hampshire.'

'Do you know why?'

She nodded. 'Yes, my father was a draughtsman in the boat-building industry and he'd just got a new job with a firm based in Hamble.'

'Are you and your brother the only children?'

'No, we have an older brother, Stephen.'

'Hmm,' he mused thoughtfully, 'that is very often the case with non-identical twins—they are the second pregnancy. What is your twin's name?'

'Richard.' She watched as he leaned forward and jotted something on a pad on the desk.

'Are both your parents alive?' he asked after a moment.

'No, my father died of a coronary nearly eight years ago,' Nicole replied quietly. 'My mother still lives in Portchester but she is in poor health—she suffers from rheumatoid arthritis.'

'How old are you now, Nicole?' He was scribbling again and did not look up.

'Twenty-seven.'

'And Stephen, how old is he?'

'Thirty-two.'

He was silent for a moment, staring at what he had written, and at that moment there came the sound of a door slamming somewhere nearby. Nicole's gaze flickered towards Louise's office and she remembered she had seen a door in the corridor marked 'Secretary'. She guessed the noise they had just heard was Louise leaving. That Louise had intended them to hear was pretty obvious. She glanced quickly at Matthew Fletcher but he was either oblivious to the fact or was choosing to ignore it.

'Are you married, Nicole?' he asked suddenly, and she jumped.

'Er, no,' she replied, feeling the colour touch her cheeks at the unexpectedness of the question.

'And your brothers—is either of them married?'

'Stephen is,' she replied, relaxing again, 'but not Richard. Stephen lives in New Zealand with his wife and baby daughter.'

'And Richard? I believe you said he was a captain in the army?'

'Yes, I did.' She was surprised he should remember. 'His regiment is serving in Northern Ireland at the moment.'

'Do you worry about him, Nicole?'

'All the time,' she replied simply.

'So your relationship is close?'

'Yes, very close,' she admitted. 'We write or phone at least once a week—sometimes more.'

'I see.' He paused, then said, 'Tell me, are there any other sets of twins in your family?'

'Yes, on my mother's side—her aunt and uncle

were twins, and there was another set—cousins, I believe.'

'Non-identical?'

'Yes.'

'Again, that is usually the case—non-identical twins repeated through the female line.' He paused again reflectively. 'Your relationship with Richard,' he went on after a moment. 'Has it always been close?'

'Oh, yes, always. . .'

'Would you say to the exclusion of other relationships, other friendships?'

She thought for a moment before replying, casting her mind back to her childhood. 'Probably, yes,' she agreed. 'We never really seemed to need other people, especially when we were children.'

'And now?' He looked up then, raising his eyebrows as his eyes met hers. 'Is there anyone special in either of your lives now?'

'No,' she replied quickly. 'At least. . .' She hesitated.

'Yes?' he prompted.

'Not for me,' she added.

'But there is for Richard?' he asked, and when she didn't immediately answer he said gently, 'Is that right?'

'Yes,' she admitted at last, and even to herself, to her dismay, it sounded reluctant. 'Yes, Richard has met someone—an Irish girl actually,' she added, desperately trying to sound casual.

'Is it serious?'

'It sounds like it.'

'And you're jealous.'

It was a statement rather than a question and she

looked up sharply. 'Of course I'm not,' she protested, 'I'm very happy for him.'

'Of course you are,' he agreed, then paused again before adding, 'but at the same time, aren't you apprehensive that your relationship with your twin might change? That you may not now be as close as you once were?'

'Well,' she began reluctantly, 'if you put it like that, yes, maybe that has crossed my mind. . .' She trailed off and looked away, unable suddenly to meet the look in his eyes, a look that seemed as if it could see into her very soul and read all her doubts and fears.

'Don't be ashamed of it, Nicole,' he said gently, 'it's a very normal reaction.' Then, leaning forward slightly across the desk, he said, 'This sort of questioning doesn't upset you?'

'No, no, of course not, Mr Fletcher,' she replied, taking a deep breath. 'I said I would help if I could. . .and I will. What else would you like to know?'

He leaned back in his chair again, narrowing his eyes. 'I wank to talk more about your upbringing—your relationships within your family unit but especially with Richard, but Nicole. . .' He paused and threw her a quick glance.

Something in the change of his tone made her tense. 'Yes?' she asked cautiously wondering what was coming next.

'While we are engaged in this work, would you please call me Matthew? It's different when we're on the ward —I know Sister Taylor likes to maintain the formalities there in front of the patients—but this is different.'

'Yes, all right,' she replied. For a split second she recalled Louise's words, then dismissed the thought, suddenly pleased that he should want her to use his Christian name and at the same time thinking just how much the name suited him.

'Right,' he said, 'so let's get on. I would like you now to try to recall your earliest memories.' He paused, and as he looked down on his notepad the intercom rang on his desk.

He gave a muttered exclamation under his breath and flicked the switch. 'Yes, what is it?' He spoke abruptly as if irritated at having been interrupted.

'Mr Fletcher, sorry to disturb you.' Nicole recognised Judith's west-country burr. 'Mr Bridgeman needs to see you urgently. I've told him you are in Theatre at two and he wondered if he could see you briefly before then.'

Matthew sighed and glanced at his watch. 'Very well, Sister. Where is he? On SCBU? Tell him I'll be right down, will you?' He flicked the switch again and glanced apologetically at Nicole.

'I'm sorry,' he said simply. 'I have to go.'

'Never mind.' She stood up, disappointed their meeting was over. 'There'll be another time.'

He didn't answer and she looked quickly at him. He appeared to be deep in thought, pulling reflectively at his lower lip. She was about to move towards the door, imagining he had forgotten she was there, caught up again in the demands of his job, when suddenly he spoke.

'What time are you off duty tomorrow?' he asked.

'Er. . .' She hesitated, for one moment caught unawares by the unexpectedness of the question. 'About eight o'clock. . .I'm on a late shift.'

'Shall we continue this discussion then?'

'Well. . .yes. . .' She began uncertainly, but he cut her short.

'But this time, I suggest we choose somewhere away from the hospital environment.' He paused and looked up at her, and she felt her pulse begin to race again. 'Do you know the Castle Inn?'

'I've seen it, in passing,' she replied carefully.

'Why don't we meet there and carry on with this over a drink—say at half-past eight?'

'All right,' she nodded. 'Half-past eight tomorrow evening it is, then.'

She felt as if she was walking on air as she left Matthew Fletcher's office. He'd actually asked her to meet him for a drink. Her own common sense told her that it was hardly a date in the conventional sense of the word because the purpose was purely to discuss his research further, but. . .nevertheless. . .!

She was so wrapped up in her own thoughts as she sped back to the nurses' station that as she rounded a corner in the corridor she collided with someone coming in the opposite direction.

'Steady on, there—where's the fire?'

'Oh, I'm sorry,' she gasped, then smiled as she realised it was Dave Burns, the porter, who was standing there, barring her path. 'Oh, Dave, it's you. I'm sorry,' she said again. 'I wasn't looking where I was going.'

'I was only thinking about you this morning.' He grinned, the smile lighting up his face.

'You were?' Nicole's eyes widened in surprise.

'Yes.' He continued to bar her way, making no attempt to allow her to pass. 'I wondered how you were getting on—how are you settling in?'

'I'm fine,' she replied, then quickly added, 'I'm gradually finding my way around and getting to know everyone.'

'It's not easy at first, is it?' he said, 'I heard someone say you'd come from up north.' As he spoke he leaned against a stretcher-trolley that was standing in the corridor, as if he had all the time in the world. 'Does that mean you don't know anyone in Hawksford?'

'That's right, Dave,' she admitted patiently, 'I don't know anyone—or rather, I didn't when I arrived but, as I said, I'm gradually getting to know people.' Suddenly, idiotically, she wondered what he would think if he knew the senior consultant obstetrician had just asked her out for a drink, then she was forced to suppress an almost hysterical desire to laugh.

'I think it would be a good idea if you were to join the hospital social club,' Dave Burns went on solemnly. 'We've a pretty good club here, you know.'

'So I understand.' She began to edge sideways, trying to squeeze past him.

'You'll join, then?' He looked eager.

'Yes, I daresay I shall. Now, I really must be getting along, Dave.'

'Eh?' He frowned. 'Oh, right, yes. I suppose I'd better get on as well. Anyway——' he straightened up, moving away from the trolley '—it's nice to talk to you, Nicole. I'll look out for you in the club—perhaps you'd let me buy you a drink sometime?'

'That's very kind of you, Dave, thank you.' She smiled and, as he moved, she hurried past him down the corridor. Two dates in the space of half an hour—life really was looking up.

She was laughing to herself as she arrived at the nurses' station.

Judith looked up from the desk. 'You look pleased with yourself,' she remarked.

'Do I?'

'Yes, like the cat that's got the cream. What's happened?'

For one moment she was tempted to tell Judith about Matthew Fletcher, but something stopped her. Her meetings with him, as she had already acknowledged, were purely business, but they could easily be misconstrued and become the source of gossip. 'I think,' she said at last, 'I've just been propositioned.'

'Really?' Judith raised her eyebrows.

'Yes, a drink in the social club, no less.'

'Don't tell me.' Judith groaned and rolled her eyes. 'Dave Burns.'

Nicole laughed. 'How did you guess?'

'It wasn't too difficult. It's fairly standard procedure whenever there's a new member of staff—it was only a matter of time.'

Nicole sighed and pressed her hand to her heart. 'And there was me thinking I was special—that it was just me he was interested in.'

'No such luck—Dave is the unit's Romeo—harmless, but quite good fun if you don't take him seriously.'

So, thought Nicole as she left the unit to go home, not only had she been asked for two dates in the space of one morning, she had also received two warnings: one that Matthew Fletcher would use her, and the other that Dave Burns was harmless provided he wasn't taken seriously. Nicole really didn't think either warning would ultimately apply to her, but neither did she let them stop her being pleased at Dave Burns's show of friendship, and excited at the thought of spending some more time with Matthew Fletcher.

Her anticipation spilled over into the following day when she found herself on edge, waiting for Matthew Fletcher to put in an appearance on the labour ward.

During report, Judith asked her to attend the delivery of Penny Rawlings, a woman of thirty expecting her first baby.

'She's in suite number three,' explained Judith. 'Her husband, Leo, is with her. It all looks pretty straightforward so far—she came in mid-morning, contractions about ten minutes apart, membranes intact. Labour is progressing satisfactorily. I gave her pethidine about an hour ago, which has helped to relax her.'

'I'll go along and get to know them,' replied Nicole. 'Anything else I need to know? Social history?'

'I don't think so.' Judith shook her head, then said, 'Oh, yes, just one thing, Leo is a solicitor and the couple are personal friends of Matthew Fletcher.'

'Gee, thanks, Judith. That's all I needed to know.' Nicole pulled a face and, as Judith grinned in response, she left the nurses' station and made her way down the corridor to suite number three.

Penny Rawlings was lying on top of the bed, desperately trying to relax between contractions. Her husband, Leo, was sitting in the chair beside the bed. He looked up as Nicole came into the room.

'Hello,' she smiled at them both. 'I'm Nicole Dennington. I'm a staff midwife and I shall be delivering your baby.'

Leo got quickly to his feet.

'It's all right, Mr Rawlings, you can stay where you are. I just want to carry out a few observations. Don't worry,' she added to Penny, who was beginning to look anxious, 'nothing more alarming than Sister Taylor was doing.'

As she was speaking, she lifted Penny's wrist and checked her pulse-rate—a quick glance at her chart had already revealed that her temperature wasn't due to be taken again for another hour.

'Are you having difficulty relaxing, Penny?' she asked, as she checked her blood-pressure.

Penny nodded, leaned her head back against the pillows and briefly closed her eyes. 'I thought it would be easy,' she said. 'But I can't seem to get comfortable.'

'I just want to check your cervix,' said Nicole. 'According to your notes, when Sister checked when you were first admitted, it was only four centimetres dilated, but you've had a vaginal examination since then, which may have helped things along a bit.'

Penny eased herself to lie down on the bed and Nicole carried out her check. 'It's nearly six centimetres now,' she said afterwards.

'Sister says it needs to be ten before things start really happening.' Penny pulled a face.

'Why don't you get up for a while?' asked Nicole.

'Get up?' Penny looked amazed.

'Yes, you may find it more comfortable to walk around during this stage.'

'Won't it hold things up?'

'On the contrary,' Nicole replied. 'Gravity very often will bring the baby's head into closer contact with the cervix and the stimulation on the nerves will help the uterus to contract even better—go with your husband.' She nodded at Leo, who looked as if he would be prepared to do anything to help ease his wife's labour. 'Walk up and down the corridor and lean on him when the contractions come.'

Dubiously Penny sat up and twisted round on the bed, then, with Leo's help, stood up and gingerly began to walk across the room.

'Don't worry,' said Nicole with a laugh. 'Nothing is going to happen just yet. I'll be back in a little while just to keep an eye on you.' As she reached the door, Penny suddenly called her back. 'Nurse, is Mr Fletcher on duty today? Matthew Fletcher?'

'Yes.' Nicole paused. 'I think he's doing a clinic at the moment.'

'He's a friend of ours,' said Leo.

It was the first time he had spoken and Nicole was quick to notice that he seemed more relaxed than when she had first come into the room. She was pleased. If Leo relaxed, it could only help Penny.

'He has agreed to be godfather to our baby,' he added.

'Well, we must try and make sure this baby puts in an appearance before Mr Fletcher goes off duty, mustn't we.' Even as she spoke, Nicole felt a little thrill shoot through her as she remembered what the end of the day's shift would mean for her. Then she tried to dismiss the thought. It was only a meeting, for heaven's sake, and nothing to get excited about, besides, she had work to do, important work, and she couldn't let personal issues get in the way.

She kept a close watch on Penny as the woman's labour progressed. Nicole's suggestion of walking around had indeed helped Penny to relax and it was over an hour later before she decided she needed to sit down. Her contractions by now were coming every three minutes and were lasting for a full sixty seconds.

Back in her room, Nicole helped Penny to wash and freshen up, then when Penny lay down on the bed again she instructed Leo how to massage her back to help ease the pain of the contractions.

Nicole was just carrying out yet another blood-pressure check when there came a brief tap and the door was pushed open.

'May I come in?' The voice was deep, slightly husky.

Nicole felt her heart leap and there was no need for her to look up to see who it was.

'Penny, Leo. How are things going?'

'Matthew!' Penny lifted her head. 'I hoped you'd come.'

'I'm afraid I can't stay at the moment, dear,' he said. 'I'll come back when I can. But you'll be in the very capable hands of Nicole. I couldn't wish for better for you.'

At his words a ridiculous surge of pleasure shot through Nicole. Common sense told her that he would probably have said that whichever midwife was attending Penny, but nevertheless, it was still nice to hear him say it.

After a brief, encouraging word with Leo and a squeeze of Penny's hand, he was gone, but his visit seemed to have lifted everyone's spirits.

Within half an hour Penny's contractions were less

than two minutes apart. 'Could I have more pethidine?' she asked Nicole.

'No, it's too close to the birth for that,' Nicole
explained 'but you could have entonox—gas and
air—to help control the pain. Would you like that?'

Penny said she would and, after using the machine
for barely half an hour, told Nicole that she felt as if
she wanted to push.

Nicole checked the cervix again. 'You're still not
quite fully dilated, Penny,' she said.

'But I need to push. . .'

'I'd like you to pant instead of pushing at this
stage,' replied Nicole.

'Like this. . .like they showed us at antenatal
classes?'

'That's it. . .' Nicole encouraged as Penny's
breath began coming in short gasps.

During the next fifteen minutes Nicole was joined
by Cathy, a pupil midwife, and Sue, a care assistant,
who were to help with the birth and, shortly after
that, Penny was ready to push.

Her contractions were not quite so frequent at this
point, but when they did come they were very
strong. Gradually she became tired with the constant
effort of pushing.

To encourage her further, with the aid of a mirror,
Nicole showed her the top of the baby's head and
this, together with Leo's continued support, per-
suaded Penny to redouble her efforts.

At last the baby's head was born, eased into the
world by Nicole, and once again Penny was asked to
pant.

As the contraction died away, Penny, supported

by Leo and Sue, was able to look down and see the baby's head.

Afterwards Nicole was not certain at what point Matthew Fletcher returned to the delivery-room. She only remembered looking up, seeing him there, but not having time to give the matter much further thought, beyond feeling pleased that he was to witness the birth of his godchild.

Uppermost in Nicole's mind was the fact that at that moment, she was in charge.

She instructed Cathy to check that the umbilical cord was not around the baby's neck, then, with Penny's next contraction, she guided first the upper then the baby's lower shoulder, then the rest of its body, from the birth-canal.

Immediately, she lifted the baby on to Penny's abdomen and looked at Leo.

'Tell Penny what you have,' she said gently.

'It's a boy!' Leo's voice was choked, and as he looked at Penny his eyes were full of tears.

Penny stretched out her arms, encompassing her baby and her husband, and for a brief moment, Nicole, Cathy and Sue turned away, leaving the little family alone for this special, intensely private moment.

Briefly Nicole allowed her eyes to meet Matthew's and she saw that he too, veteran that he was of countless births, was overcome with emotion.

Seconds later Nicole covered the baby with a dry, warm towel, and with an extractor sucked away the mucus from his mouth. She then asked Leo if he wished to cut the cord.

He hesitated. 'I don't think so,' he replied uncertainly, his voice shaking.

'Don't worry,' she smiled. 'Cathy will do it.'

Under Nicole's watchful gaze, the pupil midwife clamped and cut the cord, then, placing her hand on Penny's abdomen, Nicole felt that the placenta was ready for delivery.

Gently, with the cord, she guided the placenta through the birth-canal, then carefully examined Penny.

'I'm afraid you'll need a few stitches,' she said.

But by this time Penny was past caring. Her face was flushed and radiant as she watched Leo cradle their son in his arms and show him off to Matthew.

'Does he have a name yet?' asked Nicole, as she stepped forward and took the baby from Leo in order to examine him.

'Yes, it's Jamie—Jamie Matthew,' Leo replied. 'Jamie after my father and Matthew after his god-father,' he explained proudly.

CHAPTER FIVE

THE CASTLE INN, appropriately enough named, nestled just below the ramparts of the medieval castle. It was a popular meeting-place not only for locals but also for the many tourists who flocked to the historic town of Hawksford.

The day had been hot, the evening only slightly less so, and when Nicole arrived, it was to find the pub's roof-garden over the public bar packed with customers all seeking a breath of air.

She stood on the cobbled street below, gazing up at the wooden benches beneath coloured umbrellas, folded now with the setting of the sun, hoping fervently that Matthew had not chosen to sit in the midst of the throng. The laughter and snippets of conversation drifting down to the street reminded Nicole of the friends she'd left behind in Stockport and of the many times she'd met them in the local pub.

Quite suddenly she felt very alone.

It was the touch of a hand beneath her elbow that jolted her back to the present.

'Shall we find a quiet spot inside?' The voice was deep, slightly husky and instantly recognisable.

'That sounds like a good idea.' She only half turned her head, but as she did so caught the tang of his aftershave—a deep, musky aroma—before Matthew moved her gently forward through the main entrace of the inn and into the comparative dimness of the interior.

It was much less crowded inside and, because doors and windows stood open to the summer evening, a breeze drifted through and it appeared infinitely more pleasant than the confined space of the overcrowded roof-garden.

They found a corner alcove beneath thick oak beams, hidden from the bar by wood panelling and rich velvet drapes.

'What would you like to drink?' he asked, as Nicole sank thankfully down on to a comfortably padded bench.

'Something cold—very cold. A white wine spritzer, I think, with lots of ice.'

She watched as he moved away in the direction of the bar. He was casually dressed tonight, more casual than she had ever seen him before. In light grey trousers and an open-necked burgundy-coloured shirt with the cuffs unbuttoned and turned back, he looked younger than he did when he was on duty, boyish even, and somehow surprisingly vulnerable.

When he returned he carried her drink in one hand and a pint of beer in the other. Carefully he set both down on cardboard coasters on the polished oak table, but as he sat down himself his thigh caught the table, which wobbled precariously on the uneven flagstoned floor, slopping the contents of his glass.

He muttered something under his breath and Nicole, smiling, leaned forward, picked up the two remaining coasters and, bending down, wedged them firmly under one leg of the table.

'That's better,' she said, as the table resisted her attempts to tilt it.

The incident, insignificant as it might have been, served to banish any traces of tension there might have been between them and helped to transform the meeting from a business occasion to one of friends simply sharing a drink.

'Cheers.' Matthew lifted his glass, stared at the contents for a moment, then added, 'To Jamie Matthew, I think.'

'To Jamie Matthew,' Nicole echoed, lifting her own glass and taking a sip. 'A fine baby, if ever I saw one.'

Matthew chuckled, took a mouthful of his drink and set his glass down. 'He is rather gorgeous, isn't he? I slipped back in to see them again before I went off duty. Leo has gone home, Penny was supposed to be resting, but she can't take her eyes off Jamie.'

'They are a lovely little family.' Nicole paused. 'It's a pity it's not the same for everyone we see on the unit.'

'I agree, but life's never that simple.' He threw her a quick glance. 'Were you referring to anyone in particular?'

'I was thinking of Sharon Richards,' she said slowly.

He frowned slightly. 'The fifteen-year-old?'

'Yes,' she nodded, then said, 'I can't imagine too much joy will surround the birth of her child.'

'Sharon still has decisions to make,' he replied thoughtfully. 'Decisions that have to be made whenever a child is brought into the world.'

'But in Penny and Leo's case, I would say

decisions that were made before conception rather than after.'

He inclined his head slightly in unspoken agreement and, after a moment's silence, Nicole said, 'I understand they are friends of yours?'

He nodded. 'Yes. Penny's father was our family solicitor. He's retired now and Leo has taken his place in the law firm where he was a partner.'

'What does Penny do?' The question was quite innocent and, as Nicole waited for him to answer, she was faintly surprised to see a tightening of the muscles around his mouth.

'She owns a riding-stable,' he replied curtly.

She stared at him, and opened her mouth to ask where the stable was, to say that she was looking for somewhere to resume her riding.

But he gave her no chance, instead abruptly saying, 'Can you remember where we got to in our conversation yesterday when I was called away?'

The question was obviously intended to change the subject, and Nicole hesitated before answering, thrown by the sudden shift of topic.

In the end he answered for her.

'I know.' His tone softened as if acknowledging his abruptness. 'You were about to tell me of your early relationship with your twin.'

'So I was.' Carefully she set her glass down and took a deep breath. It was as if the earlier mood of friendship that had so briefly been established had fragmented already, and Matthew Fletcher was reminding her that this was only a business arrangement.

'How much do you remember from those early days?' he asked.

'A fair bit. What sort of things do you want to know?' She tried to sound matter-of-fact, business-like, but feared she failed miserably.

'Was Richard protective towards you?'

'From what I've heard, I rather gather it was the reverse.'

'You protected him?' He raised his eyebrows.

'Apparently so.' She smiled. 'I was a bit of a tomboy in those days. Richard, however, was a shy, sensitive child.'

'But he's made up for it since?'

'What do you mean?' she frowned.

'You said he was a captain in the army and serving in Northern Ireland?'

'He is, but that doesn't mean he's insensitive to people's feelings,' she retorted. 'In fact, I would say, quite the reverse.'

'And you still rush to defend him,' he observed.

She stared indignantly at him, then, seeing the gleam of amusement in his eyes, she sighed. 'Yes, I suppose I do,' she admitted with a rueful laugh. She fell silent for a moment as a group of young people, laughing and joking, made their way through the bar to the restaurant area.

'Do you know,' she asked when they were alone again, 'if Richard hurt himself it was me who cried, and vice versa? I can distinctly remember when I was a toddler getting myself trapped in a cupboard and bumping my head badly in trying to get out. Richard was screaming his head off. At the time I probably thought it was to summon help, but since, I've realised that it was because he couldn't bear me to be hurt. I know that, because on so many occasions since, I've felt exactly the same way if he's been hurt.'

'Has this happened when you've been apart?' he asked curiously.

'Oh, yes, many times,' she replied. 'I would get this feeling——' curling her hand into a fist, she held it tightly against her chest '—this certainty deep inside, that something was wrong with Richard, then later it would be confirmed. It usually turned out he'd been ill, or been involved in some slight accident. Once he was taken to hospital with appendicitis—I went through agonies then.'

'What was your relationship like with your parents?'

'Mine or Richard's?'

'Both of you.'

She thought, reflectively, for a moment, swirling the remains of her drink round in the bottom of her glass. 'We had lots of attention,' she said slowly at last, 'but I suppose that's pretty inevitable—twins must be very demanding—but looking back, I think Richard was my mother's favourite. . .'

'And you?'

'Oh, I was quite definitely Daddy's girl.'

He was silent for a moment, then he said, 'What about your older brother? Where did he fit in?'

'Poor Stephen,' she mused. 'I hope he didn't feel left out, although I rather suspect that must have been the case. . . Maybe that does happen with an older sibling of twins.'

He nodded. 'My research has uncovered that fact several times.'

'Your book.' She half turned to him, curious now,

and eager to know more. 'How far have you got with it?'

'It's still really in the research stage.' He seemed careful, reticent even, in the way he replied, then, more positively, he went on, 'But it's a project I've been interested in for some time and something I have promised myself I would pursue. Lack of time had always been the obstacle.'

'And you have more of that now?' she asked in surprise.

He laughed at that, his eyes crinkling attractively at the corners. 'Not so that you'd notice but I think when you really want to do something, when an idea simply won't go away, you have to find the time to do it.'

'Twins are fascinating,' she agreed. 'I guess the bond is there for life.'

'Even when one marries and the other doesn't?' he asked softly.

Something in his tone made her look up. He was watching her closely.

'I hope so,' she said quietly and, confused by the expression in his eyes, she quickly averted her gaze again.

'So do you think you're going to be happy at the Spencer Rathbone?' he asked after a moment.

'I'm sure of it,' she replied, relieved by the change of subject. 'My colleagues are nice,' she went on rapidly, then, warming to her theme, she added, 'and I shall be able to visit my mother fairly regularly, which was my main objective in moving from Stockport.'

'Are you living in digs or in hospital accommodation?' The question appeared conversational, interested without being inquisitive or probing.

'I'm sharing a top-floor flat with Judith Taylor and Mai-Lee Chang in an old house at the top of Castle Hill,' she replied, then after a pause, she said, 'How about you?'

'Me?' He was about to take the last mouthful of his pint, but he stopped and looked at her, amusement in the glance.

'Yes.' She floundered slightly, wondering what she'd said. 'Where do you live?'

He continued to stare at her, almost in surprise, as if he thought she would have known.

'I live down near the river,' he replied at last, then he stood up and, picking up both their glasses, he said, 'Let me get you another drink and you can tell me some more about your childhood.'

They stayed another hour, during which time Nicole totally relaxed in Matthew Fletcher's company and chatted easily to him, telling of her schooldays at the local primary and comprehensive schools that she and Richard had attended, and the family holidays in Cornwall and on the Norfolk Broads. She talked of their friends, and ended up even talking about her father's death—something she very rarely did—and of how badly it had affected her.

It was Matthew who eventually looked at his watch. 'I'm so sorry!' he exclaimed, 'I had no idea it was so late, I've taken up quite enough of your time,' he went on apologetically.

'Oh, that's all right,' Nicole replied happily. 'I don't mind, really I don't.'

'But you haven't even been home from work yet.'

'Never mind. My time's my own.'

'Even so.' He stood up and, almost reluctantly, she did the same. She would have been quite content to stay for another hour talking to him.

She followed him out of the inn and they stood on the cobbled street and looked down at the town, where lights were coming on in the gathering twilight.

'I'll walk home with you,' he said.

'Oh, there's no need,' she said quickly, then wished she hadn't.

'There's every need,' he replied firmly.

'But it's hardly dark. . .' The protest died on her lips.

'Even so.' He fell into step beside her and they began to walk up the hill.

'Where's your car?' She glanced round, half expecting to see the dark green Jaguar she'd seen parked in the consultant obstetrician's space in the hospital car park.

'I walked,' he replied. 'It was such a nice evening.' He paused and took a deep breath of the soft night air. 'Let's walk through the castle gardens,' he said.

'Will they still be open?' asked Nicole dubiously.

'Oh, yes, they don't lock the gates until quite late on summer nights.'

Fleetingly she wondered how he knew. Maybe, she thought, as they strolled towards the high, black wrought-iron gates, maybe he strolls here quite often on warm summer nights. She dismissed the thought immediately. If he did, it was quite on the cards he would be with someone else, and Nicole quite simply didn't want to know.

For the moment, he was with her, they had shared a drink, she was enjoying his company, he had offered to walk her home, and she didn't want to look beyond. That there would be an end to it she had little doubt, but while it was happening, she simply intended to enjoy it.

Apart from a couple who strolled beneath the canopy-like branches of a macrocarpa tree, and a man walking a golden retriever through an avenue of hydrangeas, they had the gardens to themselves.

Their footsteps made no sound on the soft, mosssy earth and the cool evening air was sweet with the scent of flowering jasmine as they made their way beneath the thick stone castle walls.

The couple disappearing through the trees had arms entwined—probably lovers, Nicole thought, and wondered if the couple had imagined that of her and Matthew. Even the thought caused a shiver to run the length of her spine, as momentarily she allowed herself to imagine what it might be like to be loved by a man like Matthew Fletcher.

'Penny for them?'

Guiltily she jumped as he spoke. 'I'm sorry?' She threw him a sharp, sideways glance and frowned.

'Your thoughts?' he prompted. 'You seemed to be miles away.'

'Oh, not really, I was just thinking about. . .' She paused, wondering what she could say. She could hardly tell him she had been fantasising what it would be like to have him make love to her! Desperately she tried to pull herself together. She really couldn't imagine what had got into her since meeting Matthew Fletcher. She couldn't remember behaving like this ever before, and certainly not over a man who was a virtual stranger. 'I was thinking about

Bridget Rose and her twins,' she lied wildly, saying the first acceptable thing that came into her head.

For one moment he looked faintly surprised, as if he didn't really believe her, then he nodded slowly. 'Yes,' he said, 'Mrs Rose is an interesting case.'

'There's nothing wrong, is there?'

'Not exactly. But I doubt she'll go full-term.'

'You expect a normal birth?'

'Probably not—but let's hope I'm wrong.'

They fell silent again, but the silence was companionable, as if each was at peace in the other's company.

They had almost reached the far side of the gardens and were approaching the boundary wall and small wicket-gate that opened on to Castle Hill, when Matthew, quite suddenly, said, 'I've enjoyed this evening.'

'So have I.' As Nicole agreed with him, her heart began to beat very fast in anticipation.

'I was wondering. . .' He hesitated, as they reached the gate and he opened it, stepping back for her to precede him.

'Yes?' she prompted softly as she brushed past him, intensely aware of his nearness.

'Would you have dinner with me one evening, Nicole?'

'Yes, Matthew, thank you. I should love to,' she replied.

'I need to check my schedule first.'

'Of course,' she murmured.

By this time they were climbing the last part of Castle Hill. 'That's where I live.' She pointed to the brick house with its red creeper.

'It looks charming.'

'It is,' she agreed. 'I was very lucky to get it. . .'
She paused, hesitating, wondering, then plunging in,
said, 'Would you like to come in? Perhaps coffee?'

'I should love to. . .but I really should be getting
home. . . I have things to do. . .'

They had stopped opposite the house, deep in the
shadows of a large sycamore cast by the glow of an
overhead street-light. . .

'Of course. . .'

'Maybe some other time,' he said softly, looking
down at her.

'Yes. . .' She trailed off, suddenly very aware of
him again, his closeness, the deep huskiness of his
voice. . .the scent of him.

He lifted his hand and touched the side of her
face. She stiffened, her instincts aroused, wondering
what he was about to do.

Very gently he ran his fingers down her cheek and
she lifted her gaze. She sensed rather than saw the
expression in his eyes, for the twilight was deepening, then, just as she found herself holding her
breath in anticipation, a light suddenly came on in
an upstairs window of the house and Matthew
looked up sharply, lowering his hand.

A figure appeared in the lighted window and
seemed to be peering out into the gathering dusk.

'It's Mai-Lee,' said Nicole, faintly ashamed by her
own irritation at the interruption.

'And I must be going.' His tone was brisk now.
'Thank you for your help. I'll see you soon.' Lightly
he touched her shoulder, but the special intimacy of
only seconds earlier had gone, evaporated into the
soft night air.

Then he too was gone, disappearing down the hill, soon to be swallowed up by the dusk.

She stood watching until she could see him no longer and could only imagine she still heard his footsteps on the cobbled street. With a sigh she turned, walked across the deserted road and let herself into the house.

Deliberately, she avoided Mai-Lee and Judith, in her state of euphoria not wanting to talk to anyone. Although she had not eaten for several hours she wasn't hungry and, bypassing the kitchen, she made straight for her bedroom.

Moments later she ran herself a warm bath, added lashings of scented cream, stripped off her clothes and stepped into the gently foaming water. Blissfully she sank down, lay back, and, relaxing, gave herself up to the sheer luxury of reliving all that had happened.

The strength of her reactions to Matthew Fletcher still amazed her—shocked her if she was honest—and even while she had, to a certain degree, exercised caution in reminding herself their liaison that evening had been purely for business purposes, even that had now changed.

It had changed at the moment he had asked her to have dinner with him, changed even further—she squirmed at the thought—when he had for that brief moment run his fingers down her cheek, that delicious moment when she had waited, anticipating more, only for him to be distracted and for the moment to be lost.

What would have happened if Mai-Lee hadn't switched on the light at that precise moment? Had Matthew Fletcher been about to kiss her? She would

never know. Now, she would have to wait and see
what happened at their next meeting.

Their next meeting—dinner he'd said. . . Where
would he take her? She had no idea. . .all she knew
was she could hardly wait. When would it be? Soon?
She wanted to see him again. Now.

A sharp thrill pierced through her body at the
thought. Was she falling in love with him? Surely
she couldn't be! Not so soon as this. There had been
others in her life, of course there had. . .other
relationships, other loves, but she'd never fallen for
anyone so quickly as this in her entire life. . .but if
she was honest, she'd never quite felt like this about
anyone before.

Restlessly she moved, realising the water had
grown cool. She should get out of the bath, dry
herself, go to bed. But what was the point. She was
sure she wouldn't sleep.

With a deep sigh she sat up, then, reaching out
for a towel stepped out of the bath. The sooner she
got to bed the sooner the morning would come.

She wanted to go to work, to be near him, to see
him again, just to be where he was.

CHAPTER SIX

To NICOLE'S surprise she slept well, awaking to bright summer sunlight and the cooing of doves from the dovecot in the garden next door. Rather less surprising was that the first thought to enter her mind was that Matthew had asked her out.

If Judith and Mai-Lee noticed her heightened state of happiness, neither mentioned it in the early-morning flurry to get to work on time.

On arrival on the unit there was even less time for gossip or speculation as the night staff told of an exhausting night with several births and ensuing complications and problems.

Penny and baby Jamie were both apparently doing well and had been moved on to the postnatal ward. As Judith began dividing the workload for the day, Nicole found herself hoping she might be asked to go to Outpatients again as she knew Matthew was due to take a clinic.

It was not to be, however, for as Judith worked her way down the list and came to her, she said, 'Nicole, I'd like you here on the labour suites, please—we have three ladies who have been admitted in the last hour. One is having her fourth child and birth looks imminent. She's in suite number five—could you assist Janice?'

'Yes, of course.' Nicole was faintly annoyed with herself for the swift stab of disappointment she felt.

If she wasn't to go to the clinic, it meant she wouldn't see Matthew until much later in the day.

As she approached room number five, Nicole heard the sound of shouting and loud, colourful language coming from within, while outside the door in the corridor a man was sitting hunched forward in a chair, his elbows resting on his knees. He was wearing a sleeveless T-shirt and grubby jeans, and as she paused in front of him she noticed his arms were heavily tattooed. One hand with the word 'love' across the knuckles was held rather awkwardly between his knees. A closer look revealed a cigarette almost hidden in the palm.

'I'm sorry, but there's no smoking in here.' She said it gently, noticing the desperation in the man's red-rimmed eyes.

'Jeeze. . .what's a bloke supposed to do. . .?' In angry desperation he took one final, frantic drag from the cigarette, then, as he tossed it on to the floor and ground it out with the heel of his Doc Marten, a further burst of loud abuse erupted from the room behind him.

'She always carries on like this,' he muttered, half apologetically. 'She were like it with the other three.'

'Wouldn't you rather be in there with her?' asked Nicole dubiously.

'No fear!' He looked up sharply. 'She won't have me anywhere near her.' He looked sheepish. 'Says it's all my fault.'

'I'm sure she doesn't mean it, Mr. . .er. . .?'

'Strong—Eddie Strong—and she does mean it. I know. . .' he added darkly.

'Oh, well, in that case,' said Nicole, 'you stay

where you are and I'll go and see what I can find out.' Suppressing a smile, she pushed open the door of room number five.

Janice, the midwife who was already in attendance, looked up in relief as Nicole approached the bed, while Maureen Strong was giving vent to yet another torrent of abuse.

'I thought I'd heard every swear-word in the book since I've been on Matty,' whispered Janice to Nicole, 'but this one is coming out with things I never knew existed—mind you, I'm not sure I want to know about some of them. . .'

'Don't you let that scumbag, Eddie, in here,' Maureen shrieked as she caught sight of Nicole. 'I warn you, I'll swing for him. . . Oh! Oh!' She gasped as another violent contraction shook her.

Janice attempted to pass her the entonox mask, but she pushed it away with such force that she knocked it clean out of the midwife's hands, it spun across the room and hit the far wall. Janice pulled a face at Nicole.

'I'm going to push!' screamed Maureen.

For the next twenty minutes she did just that, with Nicole and Janice supporting each of her legs to help her. She was a large woman and lived up to her name, almost pushing both midwives across the room in her efforts to deliver her baby.

In the end, baby Strong, in direct contrast to her mother's noisy accompaniment, slid gently and quietly into the world.

'You have a daughter, Maureen.' Nicole lifted the baby on to Maureen's abdomen.

'What!' Maureen stopped shouting and gazed suspiciously at Nicole.

'A daughter. . .look, a lovely little girl. . . She's beautiful, Maureen, fair—like her father.'

'I thought it would be another boy,' muttered Maureen, transferring her gaze to the baby as if she couldn't believe her eyes.

'Your other children are boys?' asked Janice, leaning forward and gently wiping the baby's face.

Maureen nodded. 'Yeah, all three of them,' she replied in a faintly bemused voice. 'Noisy little tykes they are, too,' she added after a moment.

'Really?' Nicole felt her lips twitch. 'Shall I tell your husband to come in now, Maureen?'

Maureen hesitated and peered curiously down at her baby again. 'Don't know what he'll make of a girl. . .' she began slowly, then added, 'Here, you take her and show him. . .' She nodded at Nicole.

'All right.' Nicole lifted the baby and wrapped her in a towel, pausing only when a final contraction shook Maureen.

'You carry on,' said Janice. 'I'll see to the placenta.'

Lingering for only one further moment, Nicole looked down at the baby in her arms, 'She really is beautiful, Maureen,' she said gently. 'Had you decided on a name?'

'No girls' names. . .no.' Maureen shook her head but her gaze remained on the baby. 'Only boys,' she added. 'It were going to be Justin. . .' She trailed off, her eyes following Nicole as she walked to the door with the baby.

Eddie was still sitting in the chair, his elbows resting on his knees, but now he held his head in his hands. He didn't appear to hear Nicole as she stepped from the delivery-room.

'Eddie,' she said softly, and he looked up quickly, his eyes widening as he caught sight of the bundle she was carrying.

'It's time to meet your daughter,' she said, and as he stood up she stepped forward.

Automatically he held out his arms and, as Nicole gave him his daughter, she noted the look of sheer wonder on his face.

'A girl. . .?' He frowned as if the very idea was totally alien to him 'We've got boys. . .'

'I know,' Nicole smiled, watching his frown gradually disappear as he gazed down at his tiny daughter, 'and won't they just be proud of their sister!'

'They will that.' His voice was suddenly husky, then he looked up sharply. 'Maureen?' he said, and Nicole noticed his eyes were bright with unshed tears.

'She's fine. . .come and see for yourself.'

He made as if to hand the baby back to her, but Nicole shook her head. 'No, Eddie, you carry her.' She opened the door and he followed her into the room, the baby cradled in his big, tattooed arms.

Maureen was lying back against her pillows and, as Nicole looked at her, she thought she detected a flicker of anxiety in her eyes as her gaze sought Eddie's.

'I never thought it would be a girl. . .' he said, his voice thick with emotion.

'What shall we call her?' asked Maureen hesitantly. 'Justine?'

'No, love.' Eddie was examining his daughter's features again. 'She has the look of my mother,' he said at last, then, looking up, said, 'I'd like to call her Alice.'

At his words Nicole glanced apprehensively at Maureen and sensed Janice was doing the same thing, but they had no cause for alarm, for Maureen nodded docilely, and said, 'Alice it is, then.'

Nicole and Janice left them alone then, Maureen and Eddie and baby Alice, and while Janice went off to get herself some coffee, Nicole made her way back to the nurses' station to arrange for a care assistant to go and help Maureen to shower and freshen up.

'Everything all right?' Judith looked up from her desk.

'Yes.' Nicole nodded, then smiled. 'A healthy seven-and-a-half-pound girl.'

'That's different for the Strongs.' Judith chuckled. 'I think Eddie was aiming for his own football team—what was his reaction?' She looked curiously at Nicole.

'He was quite overcome. . .but delighted,' she replied.

'And Maureen?'

'Speechless.'

'Well, that makes a change.' Judith pulled a face, then looked up as a care assistant approached. 'What is it, Sue?'

'Mrs Felton. Blood-pressure is raised again and there are signs of foetal distress.'

'Right, I'll ring for the obstetrician.' Judith picked up the phone and, watched by Nicole and Sue, punched out a number. The phone must have been answered quickly for Judith started speaking straight away, then, replacing the handset, she glanced up at Sue. 'He'll be up in a few minutes.' she said 'Clinic has apparently just finished.'

At her words Nicole felt her heart leap. At last she would see Matthew. Even now he was on his way up to the unit.

'Nicole, would you go along with Sue to Mrs Felton, please?' said Judith. 'I'll come along in a moment.'

'Of course.' Nicole followed Sue along the corridor—it was way past the time for her own coffee-break but, if it meant seeing Matthew sooner, she would gladly have forsaken her lunch-break, let alone coffee.

Eileen Felton, a woman in her thirties, expecting her first child, looked tired, pale and drawn. She looked up wearily as Nicole and Sue entered the room.

'Anything happening, Eileen?' asked Sue.

The woman shook her head. 'No, I seem to have gone right off the boil—I think this baby has decided it doesn't want to be born today, after all.'

'Don't worry,' replied Sue in a matter-of-fact voice. 'The obstetrician is coming up to see you in a few minutes—we'll see what he has to say, Oh, this is Nicole, she's a midwife.'

They only had time to check her blood-pressure again and rearrange her pillows to try to make her more comfortable before there came the sound of footsteps outside in the corridor.

'Ah, here he comes now,' said Sue, straightening the bedspread.

Nicole felt herself stiffen with anticipation as the footsteps stopped and the door was pushed open. For one moment she couldn't bring herself to turn to face him, to see those dark eyes with the glimmer of amusement that always seemed to lurk in their depths.

'Ah, good-morning,' said Sue. 'This is Mrs Felton.'

Nicole began to turn, to raise her eyes, then she stopped. She wasn't sure what came first, the sound of the man's voice or her first glimpse of him, the only thing she was aware of was a feeling of disbelief as she realised it was Peter Sullivan, the senior registrar, who was standing there, and not Matthew Fletcher. Her disbelief was followed rapidly by a wave of disappointment.

Where was Matthew? She watched as Peter Sullivan examined Eileen Felton. Had he taken clinic that morning? If not, why not?

'I think the best thing, Mrs Felton,' Peter Sullivan was saying, 'would be for us to take you to Theatre and to deliver your baby by Caesarean section.'

'I thought you were going to say that,' replied Eileen Felton with a deep sigh.

'Is there anyone you'd like us to contact?'

'My partner. . .he's at work, but he'll want to be here.'

'Of course. . . Nurse?' The registrar turned to Nicole. 'Can you organise that?'

'Yes.' Nicole nodded. 'I'll get the phone-trolley, Eileen, and you can tell him yourself.'

'Then, if you can prepare Mrs Felton for Theatre, please.'

With a final reassuring smile, the registrar was gone. Eileen Felton looked apprehensive and Sue began bustling around, but Nicole's mind, even while she began doing all that was expected of her, had slipped into overdrive.

Was he ill? He'd seemed all right last night. But it wasn't like him to miss clinic. Somehow she had to find out where he was.

Her casual enquiries to fellow-members of staff, however, revealed nothing. Either they genuinely didn't know where the senior obstetrician was that morning, or they weren't really bothered. And why should they be? After all, provided there was someone else to take his place for the patients, that should be all that mattered.

And to everyone else, Nicole thought desperately, that was all that mattered. Oh, why couldn't that be all that mattered to her? Why couldn't she just put him out of her mind? Forget him, get on with her work? Why, oh, why, was he playing such havoc in her life?

'Nicole, are you all right?'

She looked up sharply and saw Judith staring curiously at her.

'What. . .? What do you mean?'

'You don't seem quite yourself today. Are you feeling ill?'

'No, no, nothing like that,' she replied hastily. 'I'm just a little tired, that's all. . . I didn't sleep very well last night.'

'Oh, well, as long as that's all it is.'

As Judith moved away, Nicole let out a long breath. Judith was the one person who would probably know why Matthew Fletcher hadn't taken his clinic that morning, but for some reason Nicole was unable to ask her. Judith was far too perceptive and she wasn't sure she could appear casual enough not to raise the sister's suspicions.

In the end it was Eileen Felton who provided her

with a genuine reason to make enquiries. Minutes before the porters were due to arrive to take her to Theatre, Eileen's partner Jon waylaid Nicole in the corridor.

'Nurse, could you come a minute, please, Eileen wants to ask you something?' he said anxiously.

'Of course.' Nicole followed him into the ward and found Eileen ready in her theatre gown but looking very anxious.

'What is it, Eileen?' she asked gently.

'I understand my baby will be born by Caesarean,' replied Eileen, 'but who exactly will deliver it?'

'Why do you ask?'

'Well, throughout my pregnancy I've seen Mr Fletcher and I just wondered whether there was a chance it would be him.'

Nicole took a deep breath. 'I'll go and find out for you, Eileen,' she said with a smile. 'I'll be right back.'

Now she had a legitimate reason, she had no qualms about asking Judith Matthew's whereabouts.

'Is he in Theatre today?'

Judith shook her head. 'No, I'm afraid Mrs Felton will have to make do with Peter Sullivan.'

'Oh?' Desperately she tried to sound casual, as if she really wasn't bothered, but hoping against hope that Judith would enlighten her further.

'Yes, Mr Fletcher isn't here,' Judith went on in the same casual tone.

'He didn't do his clinic this morning, did he?'

'No,' Judith replied. 'He's attending a conference in Birmingham.'

She swallowed. 'Birmingham?'

'Yes, he won't be back until later tomorrow.'

Unaware of the impact her words would have upon Nicole, Judith disappeared down the corridor to greet a patient who had just arrived on the unit.

Birmingham! In dismay, Nicole stared after the sister's retreating form. He hadn't said. He hadn't told her that last night when he'd asked her to go out to dinner with him.

But why should he? Her shoulders sagged. What he had said when he had asked her to have dinner with him was that he would have to check his schedule first. He hadn't given any indication that he meant their date to be immediate.

What the hell was wrong with her? Angrily she turned away. She couldn't ever remember reacting in such a way as this before. But then, she couldn't remember ever meeting a man quite like Matthew Fletcher before, either.

The rest of the day dragged, and the prospect of the evening filled her with so much gloom that when Mai-Lee suggested a visit to the hospital social club, Nicole jumped at the idea—anything to help fill in the hours until Matthew's return.

Judith declined to accompany them, pleading a headache that was threatening to turn into a migraine.

The evening was warm and the pair of them walked back to the hospital.

When they arrived in the club they found a rock 'n' roll night in full swing, with a local group belting out chart-topping hits from that era.

'Just as well, Judith not come.' Mai-Lee laughed her high, bell-like laugh as they stood in the doorway and looked around, 'This not help her head. . . Oh!' she gasped, as a figure suddenly pounced on them.

'I had a feeling this was my lucky night—now I know it is.' Dave Burns, looking the part in Teddy-boy gear, beamed at them over a pint glass.

'Hello, Dave.' Nicole smiled, admiring his blue velvet-collared coat, drainpipe trousers and false sideburns.

'Come and join us—there's a little gang of us over there.' He jerked his head in the direction of the tables on the far side of the dance-floor.

'What you say?' A frown creased Mai-Lee's smooth forehead as if she feared that Nicole might not want to go, but Nicole had suddenly been caught by the catchy rhythm of an old Everly Brothers number and was happy to join in.

She grinned at Dave and they followed him through the dancers. As they approached, Nicole saw that Liz Buchanan was sitting at the table. She, too, was dressed in fifties style, with a full skirt over stiffened petticoats and with her hair back-combed into a beehive style. Her face lit up when she caught sight of Nicole.

'Hello!' she cried above the throb of the music. 'How are you? Settling in OK?'

'Yes, fine, thanks,' Nicole shouted back.

Dave disappeared to the bar to order drinks for herself and Mai-Lee, and quite suddenly Nicole felt happy. She was part of a team again, she'd made friends, and, yes, she had to admit it romance was quite definitely in the air—even if she was being forced to wait for it.

She was even happy to dance with Dave when he asked her, laughingly brushing aside his flattery and protestations of rapidly growing affection.

The whole evening was fun, but for Nicole, fun

only in the sense that it was a prelude to other, more important, events that were about to happen in her life.

The thought of those events simmered happily beneath the surface, a delicious sense of anticipation and well-being. . .so much so that, when it came, the shock was even more devastating then it might have been.

It was while she was sitting out a dance, fanning herself with a beer-mat while Mai-Lee jived with Dave.

Liz had been dancing with one of the paramedics and had just come back to the table while her partner headed for the bar.

'Phew, it's hot in here,' she said, wiping her face before sinking down into her chair. 'Is Judith coming tonight?' She glanced round as she spoke.

'No,' Nicole replied.

'I thought she would have been here—she loves this fifties stuff.'

'She said she has a headache—we did have quite a hectic day on the ward. . .'

'I see. Oh, talking of the ward——' Liz looked up quickly '—did Mrs Felton have her baby?'

'Yes,' Nicole smiled, 'a boy, by Caesarean section.'

'Did Peter Sullivan deliver him?'

Nicole nodded and Liz sighed. 'Mr Fletcher will be sorry. Mrs Felton has been waiting a long time for a baby and I know he was especially keen to deliver her.'

'I suppose that's the way it goes.' Nicole shrugged. 'He can't be on hand for all his patients.'

Liz remained silent for a moment, then she said,

'I hope he gets to deliver Bridget Rose—it's a strange thing, but he rarely seems to get to deliver twins and, what with his special interest he has, it seems a shame.'

'Yes, it does,' Nicole agreed, 'especially with the research he's doing. . .'

'You'd think he gets all the research he'd need with his own two, wouldn't you?' Liz laughed and took a sip of her drink.

At first Nicole merely thought she'd misheard, or maybe misunderstood. 'I'm sorry,' she said. 'What do you mean?'

'Eh?' Liz had turned her head to watch the dancers, but she glanced back at Nicole.

'You said you thought Mr Fletcher would get all the research he needs with his own two. . .'

'Yes?'

'But what did you mean. . .?'

Liz frowned. 'All I meant was I expect those twins of his must be a handful— let's see, they must be about twelve now, I should think—just coming up to the awkward age.'

Slowly, deliberately, Nicole set her glass down on the table. Out of the corner of her eye she could see Dave returning with Mai-Lee behind him, the patterns on her Chinese-style dress shining in the revolving disco-lights, while from the platform a Presley look-alike was telling anyone who cared to listen about his Blue Suede Shoes.

She took a deep breath. 'Are you saying that Mr Fletcher has twins?' she asked, and was surprised her voice sounded normal.

Liz had turned her head again to watch the group, and was tapping her foot to the music, and this time when she answered she didn't even look at Nicole. 'Oh, yes,' she replied, her tone offhand as if what she was saying was of little consequence, 'a boy and a girl—I daresay that's where his interest comes from . . .' She did turn then. 'Didn't you know?' she added, raising her eyebrows.

Nicole stood up. 'I had no idea,' she said, looking down at Liz and suddenly finding her beehive hair-style incongruous.

'You're not going yet, are you?' Liz looked startled.

'Yes, I think I might. . .'

Dave had just reached the table and must have heard her, for as he set more glasses down, he said, 'Of course she's not going, the night is young. Come on, Nicole, you promised me another dance.' And, ignoring her protests, he swept her back on to the dance-floor.

CHAPTER SEVEN

HE WAS married. He had children. She should have known. How could she have been so naïve?

Nicole didn't know how she got through the rest of the evening, only avoiding the prospect of Dave taking her home by phoning for a taxi for Mai-Lee and herself.

'There was no need for that,' Dave protested, swaying slightly from the amount of beer he had consumed during the course of the evening. 'I'd have walked you home.'

She was silent in the back of the taxi, only speaking to allay Mai-Lee's anxiety that it had been a mistake coming to the club.

'You not enjoy it,' the Chinese girl said miserably.

'Of course I did,' replied Nicole quickly, adding, 'I'm just tired, that's all.'

Mai-Lee seemed far from convinced, and it was with decided relief that Nicole finally shut her bedroom door and was alone with her thoughts.

She might have known he would be married—an attractive man of that age and of his status—she really should have known better, she told herself angrily, as she prepared for bed.

So what had he wanted of her? Had his offer of dinner simply been to obtain more information from her for his research? And what of that—his research, and apparent interest in the behaviour of twins? If he had twin children himself, why hadn't he acknowledged the fact? Had he deliberately with-held the information, not wanting her to know he was married?

In fact, she thought, on reflection, he had told her nothing at all about himself; all their conversation had centred on her, and her relationship with her brother.

But surely, the logical side of her reasoned, he must know she would find out sooner or later that he was married, if not from him, from hospital gossip, which only led her to believe that maybe it was an affair he was looking for.

And if it was that, simply an affair, how did she feel about it?

That he had had a powerful effect on her she was prepared to admit, and that she had begun to believe herself to be falling in love with him she had little doubt, but that was when she had imagined him to be free.

But a married man? That was a different prop-osition altogether. Nicole had worked long enough in hospitals and had seen enough relationships between colleagues, where one or both were mar-ried to other partners, to know something of the anguish and heart-break that followed such liaisons.

And in this case he had children—twins—twelve-year-olds, Liz had said. . .

Damn it, what was he playing at?

Quite suddenly, she recalled his secretary, Louise, warning her that he would use her. Was this what she had meant?

No wonder he had declined her offer of coffee the previous evening—he certainly wouldn't have

wanted to run into Judith or Mai-Lee. They might
have jumped to the right conclusions. . .

But, she agonised, was it she who was jumping to
conclusions? Had she been the one to read more
into his motives than had actually been there? Was
he simply being friendly, grateful for her help with
his research, and offering dinner to show his grati-
tude or to glean more information?

By the time she eventually fell into a troubled
sleep, Nicole had reluctantly convinced herself that
was the case, and that her intuition had been badly
wrong. Matthew Fletcher was a highly professional,
honourable man, but he was also a very married one
and she had been way off the mark in imagining that
he had any interest in her other than a professional
one.

But the following lunchtime, as she was about to
leave the house to walk to work for an afternoon
shift, the doorbell rang, and as she opened the door
her newly formed theories flew out of the window as
a delivery-man placed a dozen red roses in her arms.

The attached card, which read, 'Birmingham is
empty—see you soon,' left her in no possible doubt
as to the identity of the sender; it also clarified the
fact that it was indeed an affair he wanted.

She was tempted, she was ready to admit that.
More than tempted.

And while she worked that afternoon on the
labour suites, she even found herself wondering if
she could have an affair with him and not get too
involved.

She had almost convinced herself that maybe she
could do just that, when she heard his voice outside

in the corridor. She stiffened, immediately on guard, then moments later he came into the delivery-room where she had just delivered a baby boy.

They were oblivious to the presence of anyone else in the room as their eyes met and, as on that first occasion, when they had met as strangers, there once again was magic in the air.

In that instant Nicole knew, without any doubt, that she could never have just a light-hearted relationship with this man—for her, it would be all or nothing.

Slowly she lowered her gaze, aware as she did so of a flicker of puzzlement in his eyes, then the moment was lost as Judith began talking, the baby's mother spoke to Matthew, and the baby began crying lustily.

She avoided his gaze after that, somehow managing not to look directly at him even when answering questions he posed about his patient. It was a relief when he left the ward, but at the same time Nicole was aware of a sweeping sense of desolation.

She didn't see him again until it was almost time for her to go off duty and he waylaid her in the corridor outside the nurses' station.

'Hello.' He smiled and her heart almost stopped. 'I didn't think I was going to see you again today.'

'I've been very busy.'

'Yes.' He paused and gave her a keen look as if he found her manner disconcerting. 'Did you get my flowers?' he asked quietly at last.

'Yes—yes, thank you,' she replied, reddening, knowing her curtness sounded rude but not trusting herself to get too deeply into conversation with him.

He appeared to hesitate further, as if he too was

suddenly embarrassed, then quietly he said, 'About dinner. . .would tomorrow night be convenient?'

She longed to say yes, but she knew that if she did she would be lost. Instead, she took a deep breath and said, 'I'm sorry, Matthew, but I really don't think dinner is a good idea.'

He was silent for a moment, then softly, he said, 'Are you saying you don't think dinner is a good idea tomorrow night, or that dinner is not a good idea any night?'

'That I don't think dinner is a good idea any night.' Somehow she managed to make her reply sound firm, but the look of bewilderment in his dark eyes was almost her undoing.

'I don't understand,' he began, as a frown creased his forehead. 'I thought——'

But she wasn't to know what he thought, for Judith suddenly appeared from out of the nurses' station and almost collided with them.

'Oh, I'm sorry,' she gasped. 'I didn't see you. . .' She trailed off and Nicole became only too aware of the sister's surprise at finding them in such close confab. 'Is there anything wrong?' She glanced quickly from Nicole to Matthew, then back to Nicole.

'No, nothing.' It was Matthew who answered, a Matthew who, from the sudden change in his tone, appeared to have recovered. 'Were you looking for me, Sister?'

'As a matter of fact, yes, I didn't dare hope you were still here. Mrs Gillian McKenzie is being admitted as an emergency—do you remember seeing her in clinic?'

'Yes, I do,' he replied immediately. 'Thirty-five-year-old, first baby?'

'That's her.' Judith nodded. 'Her GP has just phoned—she's gone into early labour. She's on her way by ambulance.'

'How many weeks is she?' asked Matthew thoughtfully.

'Only thirty-three,' replied Judith, turning back to her office. 'I must get on, I'm short-staffed.'

'Would you like me to stay?' asked Nicole.

'I would be grateful.' Judith paused as Nicole spoke. 'Sue has gone home—her daughter is ill,' she explained, then added, 'Do you mind?'

'Not at all,' Nicole replied, her professionalism taking over as she pushed her personal feelings to the recesses of her mind.

Matthew went off to his consulting-room, leaving instructions that he would see the patient as soon as she had been admitted.

Ten minutes later an almost distraught Gillian McKenzie, accompanied by her husband, Derek, arrived in Maternity.

'It's too early, it's too early!' The woman sobbed uncontrollably as the paramedics wheeled her into a labour suite.

'I've delivered babies much earlier than yours,' Nicole hastened to reassure her as she helped her from the chair on to a bed.

'And were they all right?' Derek McKenzie was by now almost as anxious as his wife.

'Yes, they were fine,' replied Nicole calmly. 'In fact, I received a card from one of my pre-term babies only the other week. She wanted to tell me she is starting school after the summer holidays.'

'But it will be so small,' wept Gillian, still far from convinced.

'Maybe,' agreed Nicole, 'but if you are going to have a tiny baby you couldn't have picked a better place to do so. This hospital has a special care baby unit second to none in the country.'

'Is Mr Fletcher here?' asked Derek suddenly.

'He is,' Nicole nodded.

'Thank God,' whispered Gillian. 'I have so much confidence in him.'

As if on cue, the door opened and Matthew, accompanied by Judith, strolled in his unhurried way into the room.

He smiled at Gillian. 'I understand baby McKenzie is being impatient?'

Gillian nodded and her eyes again filled with tears.

'Well, at least all the waiting is at an end,' said Matthew kindly. 'Now, if I may, I'd like to examine you so that I can see just how impatient this little one is about making its appearance.'

Matthew's presence seemed to calm both Gillian and Derek, and Gillian's labour progressed swiftly and smoothly, until, during the second stage, while making her routine observations, Nicole discovered the baby was showing signs of distress.

Immediately she reported to Matthew, who was talking to Judith in her office.

'Would you look at Mrs McKenzie again, please?' she said.

He followed Nicole back to the delivery-room and examined Gillian once more.

'I'd like to perform an episiotomy, please, Nurse,' he said at last to Nicole and, as she turned away to prepare a local anaesthetic, be briefly explained to

Gillian and Derek that an episiotomy was a small incision to help with the delivery.

Then, as Matthew turned to the washbasin to scrub up, he murmured quietly to Nicole, 'The baby is still showing signs of distress. Resuscitation might be required—would you request Edward Bridgeman to be on hand, please?'

Nicole nodded and, as she lifted the phone and was waiting for SCBU to answer, she heard Matthew say to the McKenzies, 'I've asked Nurse to request that my colleague comes in to look at the baby as soon as it's born.'

'Why, what's wrong?' demanded Gillian, and there was a definite note of hysteria in her voice.

'I'm sure there isn't anything wrong,' replied Matthew calmly. 'But I think it might be sensible to be on the safe side and take every precaution—don't you agree?'

Derek nodded and visibly gripped his wife's hand a little more tightly. 'Mr Fletcher is quite right,' he said gently. 'It would be pointless to take unnecessary risks at this stage.'

Probably because of the sense of calm that Matthew and Nicole had established in the delivery-room, Gillian appeared to relax. And only moments after Matthew had performed the episiotomy she started to push again, and to a certain extent her anxiety over her baby was forgotten in the struggle to give birth.

Nicole found herself standing back, willing to let Matthew take over, but at the same time she found herself watching him, admiring his calm air of confidence as he encouraged and reassured both Gillian and Derek.

In the end the birth was fast and relatively uncomplicated, and Matthew immediately handed the baby, a tiny girl, to Gillian for bonding for a few seconds.

By this time, however, Edward Bridgeman had arrived to examine the baby.

'She's lovely, Gillian,' said Nicole gently, bending over the bed to take the baby from her.

'What is all this white stuff?' asked Gillian anxiously, touching the baby's skin. 'It looks like cream-cheese.'

'It's nothing to worry about,' replied Nicole firmly. 'It's called vernix caseosa, and it's there because she's so early.'

As Matthew began to peel off his latex gloves, Nicole lifted the baby, wrapped it in a green towel and turned to the paediatrician.

'It's over to you, Edward,' Matthew said with a smile, then, as his eyes met Nicole's, she felt her heart miss a beat.

Why, oh, why did he have to be married? There was such a rapport between them, had been from that very first moment—and he knew it as well. He'd given in to it, by asking her out and sending her flowers, had made it quite obvious he wanted an affair—would she, however, have the strength to resist him?

'I don't think we have too much to worry about here.' Edward Bridgeman, engaged in his examination, broke into her thoughts, jolting her back to the task in hand.

'Congratulations to you both.' He peered over the top of his gold-framed half-glasses at Gillian and Derek. 'Your daughter seems to be perfect in spite of her haste to be born. Does she have a name?' He gazed down at the baby as he spoke and she began to cry—a thin, wailing sound—and to wave one minute hand in the air.

'Yes—Lucy.' It was Derek who replied. Gillian was lying back against her pillows in total exhaustion.

'Well, I think we'll just take young Lucy down to the special unit,' began Edward Bridgeman, then, as Gillian looked up in alarm, he added, 'Just to be on the safe side and so that her mum can have some rest.'

While Matthew delivered the placenta, Nicole wrapped the baby and put her into a specially warmed crib. She had just finished when a nurse arrived from SCBU.

'Would you like to come with us?' Edward Bridgeman asked Derek.

He looked up eagerly, then glanced uncertainly at his wife.

'You go,' she said. 'Lucy must have one of us with her and I'm in no fit state yet.'

Matthew laughed. 'You will be soon. We'll get you stitched up, then I'm sure Nurse will organise a nice cup of tea. Later, you can visit your daughter yourself.'

As the paediatrician and the nurse from SCBU left the ward with baby Lucy and Derek, Nicole glanced at Matthew.

'Would you like me to ring for a houseman?' she asked.

He shook his head. 'No, I'll do the suturing myself—you organise the tea.'

It was highly unusual for a consultant obstetrician

to stay to suture an episiotomy, but Nicole was learning fast that Matthew Fletcher was no ordinary consultant obstetrician.

Even when the suturing was complete he stayed, and was sharing a pot of tea with Gillian when Derek returned from SCBU.

'Is she all right?' Gillian anxiously scanned her husband's face as he sat down beside her. He looked white and drawn and almost as tired as his wife.

'I think so. I'm not too sure.' He shrugged and looked helplessly at Matthew.

'She's in the best place,' he said reassuringly. 'She'll be carefully observed. You'll both be able to visit her a little later.'

Matthew and Nicole left Gillian and Derek shortly afterwards and made their way back to the nurses' station.

'Are you going off duty now?' Matthew asked.

Nicole nodded wearily. 'Yes, it's been a long day.'

'I'll run you home——' he began.

'No,' she said quickly, then added, 'The walk will do me good. . .'

Judith was still at her desk and she glanced up as they approached. 'Is all well?' she asked.

Matthew gave a slight shrug. 'It's a bit early to say, but it seems to be OK. The mother is fine—placenta and membranes were complete and post-partum loss was normal—the baby? Well, time will tell, but she appeared quite healthy to me. . .' He paused as the telephone rang on Judith's desk and she lifted the receiver.

Nicole had turned and was beginning to walk towards the changing-room when something in Judith's voice made her stop and look back.

'Yes, when?' she heard her say, then, 'Yes, all right, I'll warn them. Thanks, Mai-Lee.' Judith replaced the receiver and looked at Matthew, then at Nicole.

'Baby McKenzie has developed respiratory distress syndrome,' she said briefly. 'Mai-Lee says the parents should be informed.'

Nicole's heart sank and she glanced at Matthew.

Judith replaced the top on her pen and stood up. 'I'd better go and tell them,' she said.

'No,' Matthew interrupted, 'if you don't mind, Sister, I would like to tell them, and I suspect Nicole will want to go down to SCBU with them.'

'But you both should have gone off duty hours ago. . .' Judith began to protest. Before she could say any more, Matthew had turned and was walking back down the corridor.

Without a moment's hesitation, Nicole hurried to join him.

CHAPTER EIGHT

GILLIAN and Derek McKenzie looked up in alarm as Nicole and Matthew went back into the room. Nicole's heart went out to them but Matthew's manner was casual.

'Do you feel up to visiting your daughter now, rather than later?' he asked.

They both nodded but, while a look of anticipation crossed Gillian's face, her husband seemed bemused.

'Why now?' he asked, and there was apprehension in the look he shot Matthew.

Matthew replied calmly, 'Nicole and myself will be going off duty in a few minutes and we rather thought we'd like to see Lucy before we go. It hardly seems fair that we should see her again before you two, so we thought it might be a good idea if we all went together.'

'That's a lovely idea,' exclaimed Gillian. 'But I'm not sure if I can walk yet.'

'There's no question of that!' Nicole laughed, maintaining the tension-free atmosphere that Matthew had so carefully created. 'We have a wheel-chair right here for you.'

When they left the room a few minutes later, it was Matthew who was pushing the wheelchair and, as they set off down the corridor at a cracking pace, it crossed Nicole's mind that to any casual observer they made a strange picture. It couldn't be in many hospitals that the senior consultant obstetrician could be found in his off-duty hours pushing a patient through the corridors in a wheelchair—but she was quickly learning that Matthew Fletcher appeared to have his own way of doing things.

They had almost reached SCBU when Matthew, still very casually, said, 'You'll find that Lucy will be having oxygen to help her to breathe—many premature babies need this. I'm only mentioning this so that you won't be concerned at seeing the plastic box covering her head.'

By this time they had reached the big double doors of SCBU and, because Derek was occupied with helping Nicole to hold the doors open for Matthew with the wheelchair, there was no time for further questions.

Nicole was impressed with the way Matthew had handled the situation. He'd told the couple to prepare them for what they might find, but not enough to cause unnecessary alarm.

Seconds later they were enveloped by the hushed, sterile atmosphere unique to SCBU.

Mai-Lee, wearing white mask and gown, came to greet them. Her almond-shaped eyes smiled over the top of her mask.

'You have beautiful daughter, Mrs McKenzie,' she said. 'Come, I show you.' She took Gillian's hand as Matthew wheeled the chair towards the incubator where Lucy lay.

The tiny red scrap of a baby, naked apart from her nappy, lay in the incubator, her head in the perspex box into which the oxygen was being pumped. A tube had been inserted into one tiny nostril and her eyes were closed.

In spite of Matthew's relaxed preparation, a cry escaped Gillian's lips as she caught sight of her daughter.

'It's all right, Gillian,' said Nicole, bending over her while Matthew turned to Derek to offer him some reassurance.

'But—she's so small. . .so fragile. . .' Gillian's breath caught in her throat in a sob.

'She do very well,' said Mai-Lee. 'You see.'

'But why isn't she wrapped up? She'll get cold.'

'She warm in there,' said Mai-Lee. 'We watch her better without clothes.'

'I wish I could touch her. . .hold her. . .' whispered Gillian desperately.

Mai-Lee stepped forward and lifted a small flap on the side of the incubator.

'You touch,' she said. 'Through here.'

Gillian looked up in surprise as if she was afraid to do what Mai-Lee was suggesting.

'Look, like this.' Mai-Lee put her own hand through the flap and touched the sleeping baby, then, as she withdrew her hand, Gillian, after one apprehensive glance at Nicole, who smiled back in encouragement, gingerly put her own hand through the flap.

They all watched as with her forefinger she gently stroked the soft skin then, apparently comforted by the feel of her daughter, she took one tiny hand in hers and held it.

As Nicole felt a lump form in her throat, she glanced at Matthew and found he was watching her. Hastily she looked away.

When Derek, too, had made contact with his

small daughter, Mai-Lee emphasised that they could come back again in the morning to see her.

They left SCBU shortly after that, Matthew once again in control of the wheelchair, and returned to Gillian's room, where they found the night staff had come on duty and were preparing to move Gillian to the postnatal ward.

'Will you be there?' She looked frantically at Nicole as if she saw her as the only tangible link with her daughter.

'No, but I'll come and see you when I can,' she replied.

Gillian, however, looked far from happy and, as Derek shook hands with Matthew and thanked him for all he had done, Nicole recognised the growing panic in Gillian's eyes.

'Tell you what,' she said quietly, 'I'll help you pack up your things and go along to the postnatal ward with you, just to make sure you get settled in.'

'Oh, thank you.' The relief in Gillian's eyes was only too apparent as she, too, turned to Matthew and said goodbye.

It took the best part of an hour to move Gillian and get her installed comfortably in a four-bedded room on Postnatal.

While Nicole was still there, one of the staff nurses came and talked to Gillian and Derek, discussing Lucy, how Gillian would be able to feed her by expressing her milk, and establishing a rapport with them so that when Nicole left, they would not feel as if they'd been cut adrift.

The moment Nicole finally felt it was appropriate for her to go was when a care assistant brought the phone-trolley to the bedside so that the couple could phone their relatives and friends and share the news of their daughter's birth.

By the time Nicole returned to the labour suites it was late evening, Judith had long gone, Matthew too, and she suddenly realised how tired and hungry she was.

Wearily she changed out of her uniform into a pair of cream trousers and a loose tan sweatshirt, then, pausing only long enough to run a comb through her short hair, she left the unit, calling a goodbye to the night sister as she went.

As she walked out of the lift into the hospital foyer, a figure stepped out of the shadows to join her.

'I can't imagine you're going to refuse my offer of a lift now,' he said, 'not at this time of night.'

Her first instinct was to refuse, not even to contemplate putting herself into a situation where temptation would be difficult to resist. But she was too tired, too weary even to think straight, let alone fight, so she merely shrugged, the gesture signifying her acceptance of his offer.

The summer twilight was deepening as they walked from the hospital entrance to the car park. Matthew's Jaguar was illuminated in a pool of light from an overhead security-lamp. He unlocked and opened the passenger door for her and Nicole slid thankfully into the comfort of the leather seat.

Then, while Matthew let himself into the car and adjusted his seatbelt, she allowed herself to relax, leaning back against the head-rest and briefly closing her eyes.

It wasn't until they drew out of the hospital entrance and the car turned left instead of right that she felt a stab of alarm. Opening her eyes, she threw Matthew a startled glance, but his expression was set as he brought the car to a halt at traffic-lights.

'Where are we going?' she asked at last. 'I live in the other direction.'

'I know,' he replied, 'but you haven't eaten—I would imagine you must be hungry. I know I am.'

'Matthew, I said. . .' she began to protest, and he threw her a sidelong glance.

'I'm well aware of what you said, but this is different. This isn't a dinner date—this is purely and simply human survival. If I don't eat very soon I will collapse.'

She gave a helpless little shrug and, turning her head, gazed out of the window. What he said was true and she too was ravenous. Besides, what harm could there possibly be in eating together? They would probably just snatch a bar snack in the Castle Inn—it would be no different from the last time. And afterwards, she would make it quite plain that she wouldn't be going out with him again—that she wasn't interested in a road to heart-break.

But to Nicole's dismay he drove past the turning for the Castle Inn. She really wasn't dressed for dinner in a restaurant or hotel, and as he took the out-of-town route she opened her mouth to intervene.

But as if in anticipation of her unspoken question, he said, 'I know a nice little place down by the river where they serve the most delicious sausage and mash I've ever tasted.'

She found herself smiling as her fears of a grand venue were laid to rest, and weakly she leaned her head back again. There really couldn't be any harm in this.

The little place he spoke of was called Ruby's Kitchen. Situated beside the lock, it was tucked away behind a mass of willows and, Nicole suspected, would be hard to find unless you knew of its exact location.

The eating area seemed packed; the tables, with red and white checked cloths and candles in bottles, were all occupied, and to her surprise Matthew seemed well known, with several people calling out to him, smiling and eyeing her with interest.

A large, blowzy woman, her round face flushed, her dark hair drawn up into an untidy knot, suddenly emerged from what Nicole presumed was the kitchen. Her face lit up when she caught sight of Matthew and she beckoned to him to follow her.

'Come on, she'll have a table for us,' he murmured to Nicole.

Obediently she followed him to a room at the back of the building that seemed to jut out right over the river.

In the darkness Nicole could just make out the lights from the many barges moored down the stretch of river and the reflections from those same lights that shimmered and danced in the water.

'It's lovely!' she exclaimed, turning impulsively to Matthew.

'I thought you might like it.' He glanced at the woman who was hovering. 'The usual please, Ruby,' he smiled and, as she bustled away and they took their seats at one of the tables, he glanced quickly at Nicole. 'You do like sausage and mash?'

'Oh, yes.' She smiled at his apparent enthusiasm.

He quite obviously liked it here, came here often if his reception was anything to go by. Did that mean he brought his wife here. . .?

Suddenly she felt her palms go damp. She mustn't think about that now. This wasn't a date, he'd said that—it was purely a shared meal between two colleagues who had been working late.

But he had wanted to date her, he'd made that quite plain, and that to her could only mean he wanted to start an affair—she knew that sooner or later the matter would have to be faced. . .

But not now, she thought, as she faced him across the bright tablecloth—now she was weary and her hunger had increased with the delicious aromas that were coming from Ruby's kitchen.

He too seemed to have relaxed, leaning back in his chair, smiling at the girl who brought their drinks, then contentedly sipping his beer. As he set his glass down on the table and looked at her, Nicole stiffened, imagining the questions were about to start as to why she had refused his earlier invitation.

'These people fascinate me,' he said at last, looking round through the open doorway behind him. 'I envy their way of life.'

'Surely many of them are simply on holiday?'

'Some are,' he agreed, 'but many of them live on their barges.' He paused, then added, 'I hired a barge a couple of years ago and spent my vacation travelling the old waterways and canals. It was the most restful holiday I've ever spent.'

It was on the tip of her tongue to ask if his wife had enjoyed it, if his children had gone with him, but somehow she managed to bite back the words.

'In fact,' he went on, unsuspecting of her line of

thought, 'I would like to buy an old barge myself and renovate it, paint it, make it riverworthy and cruise away into the sunset. . .'

'And what of your patients?' She raised her eyebrows. 'What of all the Gillians and the Bridgets who trust and depend on you?'

He stared at her for a moment, then he laughed. 'You're quite right, I could never abandon them, neither would I be happy if I did so. No, I think my dream is one for retirement.'

'There would be nothing to stop you buying your barge,' she said. 'You could still renovate it, spend every vacation on it, and one day it would be there waiting for you. . .'

'True,' he agreed, then he sighed. 'Time, of course, is the obstacle to that. I seem to get so little to spare. Now——' he threw her a quick glance '— what with trying to compile this book, I have even less. . .and my weekends are taken up with——' he broke off as the girl who had brought their drinks appeared again with two steaming plates that she set before them.

As the girl returned in the direction of the kitchen, Nicole waited for him to complete what he had been about to say. Instead, he began to tuck enthusiastically into his food. She watched him for a moment, then, when he glanced up, as if in concern, resignedly she picked up her own knife and fork and began eating.

He had been quite right, the food really was delicious and for the time being Nicole was content simply to satisfy her hunger.

And later, as they lingered over freshly ground coffee while listening to the strains of a fiddle being played by one of the bargees in the outer room, she still felt disinclined to ask him what his weekends were taken up with, as if in some way her very omission could delay the moment of truth.

They talked instead of their work, of past experiences, then of the baby who even at that moment struggled for life in the special care baby unit, but who with every hour that passed increased her chances of survival.

'I always feel so humbled, so overawed by an experience such as that,' admitted Matthew, then, pausing a moment for reflection added, 'And that feeling doesn't become diminished by the number of times it happens. I still, after all this time, feel so helpless at the anguish in the parents' eyes when they expect us to perform a miracle.'

Nicole nodded. There was no need for words; she knew only too well what he meant.

When they finally left Ruby's it was very late and they were among the last to leave, strolling, unhurried now, not straight back to the car but on to a small wooden landing-stage on the river, lit by one solitary light that served as a guide to approaching craft.

They were silent for a long while, leaning on the wooden parapet watching the reflection of lights from the barges, the only sounds the gentle lapping of dark water against the supports of the landing-stage and occasional rustlings in the reeds on the far bank.

In the end it was Matthew who spoke. 'I've enjoyed tonight,' he said simply.

'Yes,' she agreed, surprised to find that her tiredness had vanished.

'Just as I enjoyed the other evening we spent together.'

'Me too,' she admitted at last.

There was a long silence. 'And yet you weren't keen to repeat the experience?' He turned his head at last to look at her.

'No.'

'May I ask why?'

She hesitated. How was she to answer such a question? In the end she said, 'I couldn't make up my mind what you wanted.'

'I don't understand.' She sensed rather than saw the frown that creased his forehead. 'I wanted us to spend time together, not just in a work environment, but so that we could get to know one another better. There's something between us, Nicole,' he said softly, and as she caught her breath he went on, more urgently now, 'It was there from the moment we saw each other in town—I know it, and I think you do too.'

As he was speaking he turned, then moved closer to her and she became intensely aware of his nearness. She knew what was going to happen, knew his arms would go around her, knew also that she should resist him, could quite easily be lost if she gave in to temptation.

But as his lips closed over hers she lost all power to resist, was swept along on a tide of desire, desire so strong that it threatened to overwhelm her. In a purely spontaneous gesture she allowed her arms to slide around his neck, her fingers to sink into the dark hair as she responded to his kiss.

And his kiss was all she had imagined it would be: both tender and passionate.

'There,' he whispered, as at last they drew apart, 'you can't deny it now, not after that.'

No, she couldn't deny it, was almost powerless to resist it. . .but that still didn't make it right.

With an almost superhuman effort she tore away from his arms and stood holding on to the parapet, trying desperately to control herself.

'Nicole. . .what is it? What's wrong?' She could hear the bewilderment in his voice.

'Why didn't you tell me?' she blurted out at last.

'Tell you what?'

'When we were talking, about Richard and me. . . why didn't you say you had twins of your own?'

The pause before he answered was only marginal. 'I didn't see the need to. It was your relationship with your brother I was wanting to research—I don't need to research my own children, I know all about them.'

'But I didn't even know you had any children.'

'You didn't?' He sounded genuinely surprised, then gently he added, 'It needn't make any difference.'

In desperation she stared at him in the darkness, unable to make out his features or to see the expression in his eyes. From what he was saying it sounded as if he was quite prepared to embark on a full-scale illicit relationship, and hang the consequences.

'Nicole,' he said softly at last, then, reaching out, he touched her cheek.

She jumped, shying away from him in alarm, then suddenly something seemed to snap inside her.

'Matthew, I'm sorry—I don't want this to continue any further—it must stop right here. I've always drawn the line at having an affair with a married man and I don't intend to change things now.'

He gave a low exclamation, but she hurried on, not giving him the chance to say anything.

'I happen to believe this sort of thing always leads to heart-break for someone. . .'

'Nicole —— ' he said gently.

'If not for the wife, then for the other woman. . .'

'Nicole——'

'And the children always suffer, I don't care what anyone says. . .'

'Nicole, will you please listen to me?'

Suddenly she realised he was laughing, and she felt a surge of anger that he could be treating the whole thing so lightly when it had already caused her such pain.

'Maybe you think it all harmless fun, this sort of thing, but I've seen enough to know it might start out that way, but it very soon ends up——'

Her outburst was finally silenced as for the second time he brought his mouth down on to hers. This time, however, his kiss was firm, decisive, and left her gasping.

When he lifted his head at last he held one hand firmly over her mouth. 'Now, will you let me speak?'

Helplessly she stared at him in the darkness.

'You thought I simply wanted an affair?' he said, then, because she was powerless to answer, he shook his head, 'Ah, Nicole, is that all you thought of me?' He took his hand from her mouth.

'What was I to think?' She continued to stare at him. 'You deliberately withheld the fact that you had children, so I can only believe you also deliberately withheld the fact that you have a wife.'

In the silence that followed, a bird rose from black clumps of reeds on the opposite bank, flapped its wings, uttered a low, desolate cry and flew away downstream.

'Nicole,' he said at last, 'I'm sorry, but I assumed you knew. Everyone else at the Spencer Rathbone does. My wife is dead—she was killed in an accident five years ago.'

CHAPTER NINE

She stared at him in astonishment, then with a little cry she turned away.

They remained silent for a long while as Nicole battled with a variety of emotions, then at last she turned back to Matthew.

'I'm sorry,' she whispered, 'so very sorry. I had absolutely no idea—no one said anything at all.'

'Why should they?' He shrugged slightly. 'As I say, I suppose they simply thought you knew. Didn't you say anything to Judith Taylor?'

'What do you mean?'

'About the rapport between us? Or about the fact that you've been helping me with research?'

'No.' She shook her head. 'In fact, I'd come to the conclusion that one of the reasons you didn't come into my flat for coffee the other night was in case you were seen by either Judith or Mai-Lee and there would be speculation and gossip.'

He laughed then, a low chuckle. 'If you remember rightly, I told you at the time the reason I didn't come in was because I had things to do—one of those things was picking the twins up from a friend's house.'

'Oh, Matthew!' She didn't know whether to laugh or cry, but at the same time the glorious truth was slowly dawning. He wasn't married! He was a free man—a widower. 'Tell me about them,' she said impulsively, reaching out and putting one hand on his arm. 'These twins of yours—I want to know.'

'What do you want to know?'

'Everything—what are their names, how old are they?'

He laughed again but sounded pleased that she should be interested. 'Their names are Ashley and Sara and they are nearly twelve years old. They attend school here in Hawksford.' He hesitated for a moment, then added, 'I considered that was essential—it's enough that they don't have a mother, let alone a father whom they never see.'

'How do you cope when they're at home and you have to work?'

'We've had two or three housekeepers over the years and various child-minders and help from grandparents, but mostly it's just me and them. . .' He trailed into silence, then thoughtfully said, 'Would you like to meet them?'

'I should love to.' Her reply was spontaneous, unhesitating.

'And will you now reconsider that dinner date?'

'Of course.' She laughed, the excitement bubbling up inside her as she realised yet again that what she had thought of as being impossible was now a reality.

'In that case, may I suggest I pick you up tomorrow night around seven o'clock and we go first to my home to meet the twins.'

'That will be wonderful—I can hardly wait.'

With a sound like a low groan, he pulled her almost roughly into his arms again and brought his mouth down to cover hers.

A sweet shaft of desire shot through her as,

fervently, with her pulses throbbing, she responded to his kiss.

And gradually, as she felt the warmth of his hard body, she knew she wanted more. She wanted him to love her, to carry her away to finish what he had started, to satisfy the clamourings deep inside her own body.

Instead, he seemed to tear himself away from her, albeit reluctantly and as if he was fighting for control.

'I must take you home,' he murmured, almost distractedly.

Again she sat beside him in his car as he drove back into the town and, as before, her thoughts were in turmoil, only this time it was a different sort of turmoil—this time, her senses and desires were aroused and were begging for release.

As he drew up in front of the house he left the engine running.

She threw him an apprehensive glance. 'Is it any good me asking you in for coffee tonight?' she asked.

Ruefully he chuckled and shook his head. 'I really do have to get home. The twins will be wondering where on earth I've got to, and besides——' he took one of her hands in the darkness and held it to his lips '—if I were to come in now, I couldn't be held responsible for what I might do. Just think what your flat-mates might make of that.'

'I'm not sure I would care,' she whispered, tightening her own grip on his fingers.

'But I would,' he said firmly. 'I would hate there to be any gossip about you at the hospital.'

Moments later she watched as the Jaguar slid away down the hill. There was something charmingly old-fashioned in his concern for her reputation, she thought ruefully, but at the same time it did little to assuage her desires.

With a little sigh she turned and, feeling as if she was walking on air, entered the house.

The hall was in darkness, but as she closed the front door a light came on at the top of the stairs and Judith called out.

'Is that you, Nicole?'

'Yes,' she replied happily as she began to climb the stairs.

'Oh, I heard a car. . . I thought.'

Nicole only hesitated for a moment. 'Matthew Fletcher gave me a lift home.'

'Good grief!' Judith peered at her as she reached the top of the stairs. 'Have you been at the hospital all this time?'

'No.' Nicole laughed and shook her head. 'We went for something to eat when we left work.'

Judith's jaw dropped. 'Matthew Fletcher took you for something to eat!'

'Yes, what's wrong with that? He is human, you know, he does have to eat the same as the rest of us.'

'Well, yes, I know, I was surprised, that's all—he doesn't make a habit of taking the staff out, you know. With the exception of Louise, I can't remember him taking anyone else out.'

She had been about to go into her bedroom but she stopped, one hand on the doorknob. 'He wasn't exactly taking me out, Judith, it was simply that it was very late by the time we'd left SCBU and we were both hungry. . .' she paused. 'What did you mean about Louise?'

'Louise?' Judith mumbled absent-mindedly. She had turned away and was fiddling with the red roses, which the previous day Nicole had arranged in a vase and placed on the landing table.

'Yes, you said with the exception of Louise. . .'

'Oh, that. . .yes.' She shrugged. 'Well, he often took Louise out.'

'Really?' Nicole tried to sound casual but her heart had lurched and seemed to drop into her stomach. 'I didn't know they were an item.'

'Oh, they aren't now—it all ended very suddenly, then the next thing we heard, Louise was leaving— no one really knows quite what went wrong. Hadn't you realised that?'

Nicole shook her head, then gave a short laugh. 'No. The trouble is, when you're new to a place, people assume you know everything that's going on, and you don't—far from it. In fact. . .' She paused briefly. 'I didn't even know that Matthew Fletcher had twins—let alone that he was a widower,' she added quietly.

Judith looked up sharply and stared at her. 'Oh, dear,' she said. 'Yes, I suppose I did just assume you knew—it never even occurred to me to tell you—it's such common knowledge.' She paused, her eyes narrowing, then said, 'Don't go to bed yet, Nicole, come and have a chat—do you fancy a coffee?'

Nicole hesitated, then with a slight shrug said, 'Yes, all right.' Following Judith into the kitchen, she watched as she filled the kettle. She was tired and if she was honest would have preferred to go to bed, but there was a part of her that was still curious, that needed to know more.

'Have you met the twins?' she asked after a moment.

Judith nodded. 'Yes, a couple of times. Matthew has brought them into the hospital at Christmas.'

'What are they like?'

'They seem nice enough children, rather quiet, I thought.'

'Did you know their mother?' Nicole asked, as Judith spooned two heaped teaspoonfuls of coffee into a couple of mugs.

'No.' Judith shook her head. 'She died before I joined the unit—but from what I've heard, she was a very striking-looking woman.'

'He must have had a difficult time bringing the twins up on his own.'

'Oh, I shouldn't feel too sorry for him.' Judith poured boiling water into the mugs, added milk, handed one to Nicole and went on, 'With his money, he can afford the best in child-care.'

'It can't be the same as a mother—money isn't everything.'

'Maybe not.' Judith gave a short laugh. 'But it sure does help. Do you know where he lives?'

'Not really, only that it's near the river.'

'Is that what he told you?' Judith laughed again. 'Well, I suppose in effect that was right. He has one of those beautiful properties on the other side of the bridge, whose gardens back on to the river.' She took a mouthful of coffee. 'Oh, I don't doubt he's earned it,' she reflected, then, after a moment, added, 'All I'm saying is that wealth-and status can go a long way to overcoming personal difficulties.'

Nicole remained silent, not at all sure she agreed with Judith, more of the opinion that nothing could really make up for the loss of a parent to two young children.

Something also made her refrain from telling Judith that she was to meet those same children the following evening before going out yet again with their father.

She didn't feel she could cope with the renewed speculation in Judith's eyes, which would be sure to be there when she realised there was more to Nicole's relationship with the consultant than she had at first led her to believe.

Instead, she talked of other things; of baby McKenzie and her chances of survival, of other hospital matters, then, finishing her coffee, she drained her mug and stood up.

'I must get to bed.' She yawned and, crossing to the sink, rinsed her mug under the tap and set it in the rack to drain. 'Another full day tomorrow.'

'Yes, for me too,' agreed Judith, but she made no attempt to move, her elbows on the kitchen table, her chin resting on her hands.

Nicole had reached the door, had said Good-night, when Judith, casually, quietly, said, 'Lovely roses—they look beautiful in the copper vase.'

She froze, one hand on the doorknob, then, swallowing and without turning, said, 'Yes, they are lovely.'

'They must have cost a fortune. Someone must think a lot of you, but maybe it's someone wealthy. . .' Judith trailed off, then, when Nicole remained silent, she said softly, 'Be careful, Nicole.'

'Of course.' She turned then, defiantly tilting her chin and allowed her gaze to meet Judith's. 'I'm not a child, I'm quite capable of looking after myself.'

'Fine.' Judith stood up and moved to the sink. 'I would hate to see you get hurt—that's all.'

Nicole fled after that to the sanctuary of her own room to try to unravel her emotions.

Why should Judith think she would get hurt? It was pretty obvious she had guessed who the roses were from, just as it was pretty obvious she had guessed her feelings for Matthew.

But why should she assume he would hurt her? He was, after all, a free man. He was older than she was, it was true, but she'd always been drawn to older men and to Nicole that didn't present a problem. Judith had also confirmed her earlier suspicion that Louise had had a relationship with Matthew. But that, apparently, was over, so she had nothing to fear on that score.

As she prepared for bed, however, flinging her curtains open to the warm summer night and the gentle murmurings from the dovecot, she once again recalled Louise's warning. 'He'll use you,' she'd said. But what had she meant?

Surely, thought Nicole as she turned from the window, it was merely a case of sour grapes: the secretary, peeved that her own relationship with Matthew was at an end, had seen the rapport between the two of them and had done her best to put an end to it.

But whatever it was, she was determined not to let it blight her newly found happiness. Matthew had made it perfectly plain that he was attracted to her and that he wanted more to come of their friendship. If he didn't, then he would hardly be going to the trouble of taking her to meet his children.

It was with that thought uppermost in her mind that Nicole finally fell asleep.

The following morning she was in the same euphoric state; when she wasn't longing for a glimpse of Matthew, she was counting the hours until the evening, when they could be together.

She found herself avoiding any personal conversation with Judith—she was unable to explain why, even to herself, but she imagined she detected a faint air of disapproval, even to the extent that Judith didn't ask her to do the clinic that morning when it should have been her turn to do so.

It almost seemed to Nicole as if the move was deliberate, to prevent her having too much contact with Matthew. If that was the case, she was uncertain why, but she shied away from discussing it with Judith or even voicing her suspicions, as if Judith might tell her something to destroy her happiness.

It was towards the end of the morning, when she was attending the rather difficult and prolonged labour of a young woman expecting her first baby, when someone knocked on the door of the labour suite. Sue, who was assisting Nicole, called out, the door opened and Michelle, a new care assistant, cautiously peered round the door.

'Nicole,' the girl said hesitantly, 'Sister Taylor would like a word with you.'

Nicole glanced at Sue. 'Can you cope for a moment?'

'I should think so.' Sue smiled at the patient. 'It doesn't look as if baby is in too much of a hurry to be born.'

Nicole joined Michelle, who was waiting for her

in the corridor, and together they began walking to the nurses' station.

'How are you settling in?' Nicole asked the girl, mindful of how she had felt when she had first joined the unit.

'Not too badly.' Michelle pulled a face. 'It's all a bit strange—I keep getting lost.'

'You're bound to feel strange at first—I know I did, but don't worry, you'll soon get used to the place.' She hesitated, then, throwing the girl a sidelong glance, she said, 'Did Sister Taylor say why she wanted me?'

Michelle shook her head. 'Not really, but I think it might be something to do with the antenatal clinic.'

Nicole felt her heart skip a beat—the clinic meant Matthew. But there was no chance for further speculation as by that time they had reached the nurses' station.

Judith was sitting at her desk and, as they approached, Nicole thought she looked harassed.

'Oh, good, there you are,' she said as she caught sight of Nicole. 'We've got a bit of a problem, and it appears you are the only one who can help.'

'Me?' Nicole's eyes widened. 'I don't understand.'

'It's Sharon Richards.' Judith lowered her voice and glanced over her shoulder towards a small room they used for interviewing.

'Sharon. . .?'

'Yes, she apparently turned up in the clinic this morning without an appointment and is saying she won't go until she's seen you.'

'But. . . I hardly know her, I've only seen her the once when she was booked in.'

'Maybe so, but she told Liz that you'd told her she could come and talk things over at any time.'

'Well, yes, but what I meant was——'

'Then Mr Fletcher got to hear about it,' Judith continued rapidly, not giving Nicole a chance to answer, 'and he insisted that she come up here and talk to you. . .said you were the one to sort things out. . .'

Nicole felt her cheeks grow warm under Judith's gaze.

'Well, in that case,' she muttered, 'I'd better go and get on with it. Where is she? In there?' She inclined her head in the direction of the interview-room and, when Judith nodded in reply, she strode past her and pushed open the door.

The girl was sitting by the window. She looked up sharply as Nicole entered the room, and the mutinous expression on her sullen little face eased into one of relief.

'Good,' she said, flicking back her blonde hair. 'They've been trying to fob me off, but I wasn't having any of it—I told that silly cow in the clinic I wasn't budging until I saw you.'

'Why did you want to see me, Sharon?' asked Nicole, feeling her lips begin to twitch and wondering how Liz had reacted to this stroppy young woman.

'You said I could come and talk when I wanted.'

'Yes, I did,' agreed Nicole, shutting the door behind her.

'Well, I want to talk, now. You're the only one in this place who seems to understand.'

'What about Mr Fletcher? Wouldn't he understand? I thought you got on well with him.'

'I do, but he's a man, and let's face it, how can they know how we feel? They don't have babies, do they?'

'No, Sharon,' agreed Nicole solemnly. 'They don't.'

'It's about what I'm going to do afterwards,' Sharon went on in the same defiant tone.

'I thought you had decided on adoption.'

'I thought I didn't have any other choice, but now, well, I don't know, that's why I've come to see you.' Sharon sniffed. 'Something's happened—well, two things, really.'

'Tell me about them.' Nicole perched herself on the edge of the table.

'Well, first of all Jason came back.'

'The baby's father?'

'Yeah. He hadn't cleared off because of the baby. It was because he was in trouble with the police. It's sorted now. He wants us to get together when I'm sixteen.'

'And how do you feel about that?'

'I dunno, really.' Sharon frowned and shrugged.

'You said two things, Sharon—what was the other?

'Me dad's got a job—security guard—it's a good job and me mum's giving up at the biscuit factory. She says if I want to keep the baby she'll look after it, so that I can do me hairdressing training.'

'And what would she think about you getting back with Jason?'

Sharon shrugged again. 'Goodness knows. I suppose she'd get used to it in time—he's on probation now, but he's starting a training course to be a plumber. . . I don't know what to do.' She looked up at Nicole in sudden, helpless desperation.

'What do you want to do, Sharon?'

'I want to do me training. . .'

'Yes. . .and the baby? Do you want to keep it?'

'I think so. . .' She hesitated, clearly unsure how to go on, then, as if finally reaching a decision, she said, 'Yes, I do. I didn't at first, it didn't seem like it was happening to me. . .but lately. . .' as she spoke, she moved her hands across her stomach in a protective gesture. 'It's been different.'

'You've felt the baby kicking?' asked Nicole gently.

'Yes.' Sharon's voice dropped to a whisper. 'All the time, but especially late at night when everyone else is asleep, then it's just me and him. . .you know? I don't think I would be able to let him go to anyone else.'

'You think it's a him?' Nicole smiled.

Sharon nodded and her expression was serious, as if she didn't just think it, but that she was certain her unborn child was a boy.

'Have you mentioned this to your social worker?'

'No, I daren't.' Sharon looked up sharply. 'She'll flip her lid. She thinks it's all decided—the adoption and all that.'

'You're perfectly within your rights to change your mind at this stage, Sharon,' said Nicole evenly. 'I think you should tell your social worker what you've told me.'

Sharon remained silent for a long moment, kicking at the leg of the table with the toe of her scuffed white sandal, then slowly she lifted her head and looked up at Nicole from beneath the heavy fringe of her hair. Before she spoke they both heard the sound of a baby crying in the ward across the corridor.

'Would you do it?' she said at last, her tone pleading.

Nicole took a deep breath. 'Very well,' she said. 'Stay there. I'll go and see if I can phone her.'

The look of relief on Sharon's face was only too obvious as Nicole eased herself off the table.

It was a comparatively simple matter for her to phone the hospital social worker and explain the situation, and she was back within ten minutes.

'That was quick!' Sharon looked up in disbelief. 'Did you speak to her?'

Nicole nodded. 'Yes, you've nothing to worry about, Sharon.'

'What did she say?' The girl looked suspicious, as if she was totally unused to anything being so simple or straightforward.

'She said she quite understood, but there was just one thing she wanted you to do.'

'What's that?' Sharon's eyes narrowed suspiciously.

'Simply to let her be there when you tell your mother of your decision.'

Sharon frowned and wrinkled her nose.

'It's in everyone's best interests—she'll work closely with you all,' Nicole went on firmly.

'Yeah, all right.' Sharon gave a deep sigh, stood up and walked towards the door, then she stopped and looked back at Nicole. 'Thanks,' she said.

'That's OK, Sharon—any time you want to talk.' Nicole followed her from the room and Judith glanced up at them both from her desk.

'Everything all right?' she asked.

'Yes, fine, thank you, Sister,' Nicole replied. 'Sharon is just leaving. I'll see her to the lift.'

They walked across the reception area just as the lift arrived. As the doors opened Dave Burns stepped out. His face lit up when he caught sight of Nicole.

'Goodbye, Sharon—see you soon.' Nicole smiled encouragingly at the girl as she stepped into the lift. The doors closed, the lift began to descend to the ground floor and Nicole turned to Dave.

'You know, Nicole,' he said with a grin, 'if I didn't know better, I'd say you've been avoiding me.'

'Oh, Dave, as if I would!' Nicole pulled a face.

'Prove that you haven't, then,' he demanded.

'What do you mean?' she protested laughingly. He fell into step beside her as she began to hurry back to the labour suite.

'Come to the club with me tonight.'

'Tonight. . .?' At the thought of the evening to come with Matthew, a shaft of pleasure pierced through her. 'Oh, Dave, I can't. . .'

'No excuses, or I will think you've been avoiding me,' he said firmly. 'Besides, it's a seventies night—just think, all that flower-power, mind-blowing experiences. . .free love. Don't forget the free love, Nicole—we could have a whale of a time. . .'

'Dave, I'm sorry.' She was laughing openly now as they stopped outside the delivery-room. 'I'm not averse to a bit of hippy-style culture,' she said, 'but I really do have another engagement.'

'You'd look wonderful in a caftan.' With a sigh, Dave leaned on a stretcher-trolley and gazed deeply into her eyes. 'I think you should drop this other guy, whoever he is, and come and enjoy wonderful happenings with me.'

'Who says there's another guy?' She raised her eyebrows.

'No one has to,' replied Dave softly, all traces of amusement gone now, 'it's in your eyes.'

'Oh, nonsense!' She laughed, raising her hand in a dismissive little gesture.

'It's not nonsense at all—I know these things,' he said seriously. 'And I tell you what—he's a very lucky guy. I only hope he knows it. . .' He trailed off, then gave another sigh, 'You do realise, Nicole, you've broken my heart. . .'

She stared at him, uncertain for one moment whether he was joking now or not.

'But,' he went on after a moment, 'if you should change your mind, you know where to find me.' He winked at her then, straightened up, and without a backward glance, sauntered off down the corridor. Before he turned the corner she heard him whistling a hit tune from the seventies.

She watched him for a moment, then, with a smile, she turned and entered the delivery-room where she found the baby, who earlier had been so reluctant to put in an appearance, was apparently now changing its mind.

CHAPTER TEN

MATTHEW picked her up a little after seven and, as she slipped into the passenger seat of the Jaguar, Nicole couldn't fail to notice the admiration in his eyes.

She had dressed with great care that night, choosing the sand, stone and tan colours that went so well with her olive complexion, while her dark hair, freshly shampooed, fell in its sleek, shiny bob, framing her face.

'You look lovely,' he said simply as she fastened her seatbelt.

'Thank you.' She tried to keep her answer light, casual, but her heart had leapt at his words. From the look in his eyes she knew this had been no idle compliment—he had really meant it.

The car drew smoothly away down the hill, gathering speed, and when she guessed all his concentration would be centred on the junction he was approaching, she attempted a sidelong glance at him.

Tonight, he wore a black polo-necked shirt together with a lightweight, sand-coloured jacket and trousers and a pair of Italian leather loafers. He looked both stylish and relaxed. There was something intensely masculine about Matthew Fletcher: his rugged, unconventional looks, his undeniable charm and the way the short dark hairs on his wrists below his cuffs were tipped with gold. Nicole felt a shiver of excitement.

'I've told the twins I'm bringing you to meet them.' He broke into her thoughts.

She gave a little start. 'What did they say?'

'I'm sure they are looking forward to meeting you.'

'Do they know I'm a twin?'

'Not yet.' He grinned. 'I was saving that particular piece of information.'

'Tell me a little more about them.' Suddenly she felt she needed to know something about these children of his, anything, even if it was only to provide a talking-point.

'What do you want to know?'

'I don't know. . .what are their hobbies, interests? What are they into?'

'Well.' He paused reflectively. 'Ashley plays rugby and is a whiz-kid on his computer.'

'And Sara. . .?'

'Ah, Sara,' he mused. 'In some ways Sara is a strange child. I think her mother's death affected her very deeply. At the time, I thought it was Ashley who suffered the most, but since, I've come to the conclusion it was Sara who sustained lasting damage.'

'So what are Sara's interests?'

He didn't answer immediately, and when she threw him a glance she saw his mouth had tightened. Then he said quietly, 'She is obsessed with horses and riding.'

Nicole frowned. 'You said that as if you are surprised. I would have thought that is the passion of many eleven-year-old girls.'

He didn't reply. Instead, quite casually, he said, 'Do you ride, Nicole?'

'Yes.' She nodded. 'Richard and I used to ride regularly at a stables near Hamble. But I must admit, I've not had much opportunity recently. It was one of the things I thought I might be able to resume now that I'm living in Hawksford. Does Sara have her own horse?'

Matthew shook his head. 'No,' he said shortly, 'she doesn't.' Then, abruptly changing the subject, he said, 'Did Sharon Richards come to see you this morning?'

By now, they were approaching the large houses on the outskirts of town whose gardens backed on to the river.

Nicole had been looking at the houses with interest, wondering which one was Matthew's, but she half turned her head at his question.

'Sharon?' she said in surpise. 'Yes, she did.'

'Can I assume,' he went on, 'she's changed her mind about giving up her baby for adoption?'

'How did you guess?'

He smiled. 'It wasn't too difficult—I know the signs. I found it touching, though, that she was only prepared to speak to you about it.'

'So did I,' admitted Nicole. 'I'd only met her once before.'

'You must have made a deep impression on her.'

'I only hope I gave her the right answers to her questions.' Nicole felt her cheeks grow warm at the note of admiration in his voice.

'I shouldn't think there's too much doubt about that.' As he was speaking, he signalled left and drew into the driveway of a large house set well back from the road and almost hidden from view by the foliage of several cherry-trees that dotted the lawn.

'Here we are,' he said easily, bringing the car to a halt, its tyres crunching on the loose gravel drive.

He switched off the engine, got out of the car and walked round to open the passenger door. As Nicole alighted, she looked up at the house.

It was built in the same mellow red brick as the house where she lived, but its upper storey was clad in the same terracotta tiles that covered the roof. The small panes of glass in the many Georgian-style windows glinted in the evening rays of the sun, while the heavy oak door stood invitingly open.

'Welcome to Chandrapur House,' he said, taking her arm.

'That's a very foreign-sounding name for such an English-looking house,' she said, mystified.

'The house was built by my late wife's grand-father,' he said, then added, 'he was a diplomat in India.'

He stood aside for her to precede him into the spacious hallway, and as he did so she was struck by a sudden pang as she realised how little she knew about this man.

The house was very quiet, too quiet to be the home of two eleven-year-old children. The hallway opened into several large rooms that led into each other through a series of archways. A light peach fragrance hung in the air, while the fabrics and furnishings were of soft, muted colours and clean uncluttered lines: deep floral sofas, rich, dark wood and book-lined walls.

There was no sign of the children, the only welcome being from an elderly springer spaniel lying on the hearthrug, who lifted its head at their approach and thumped its tail in greeting.

'Hello, Monty, old fellow.' Matthew crouched down and fondled the dog's ears. 'Where is everyone?' Straightening up again, he turned to Nicole and said, 'My housekeeper, Sadie, must be in her room, but I don't know where the children are.'

He walked to the French windows that stood open to the warm summer evening and looked out as if he expected to see the children outside, then impulsively he turned back to Nicole. 'Come and have a look at the garden,' he said.

Enclosed by a wall of the same mellow brick as the house, the gardens were quite enchanting, with deep herbaceous borders packed with the misty blues, purples and lilacs of lavender, delphiniums and lupins, surrounding immaculate lawns and rose-beds.

'We have two fish-ponds,' said Matthew, pointing to a corner on the far side of the lawn, 'and over there by that gate in the wall is our herb-garden— I'm rather proud of that.'

'I had no idea you were a gardener.' Nicole gazed round in delight, her eye coming to rest on a pergola whose rafters were covered by tumbling cream roses, then a distant corner where glimpses of an orchard were visible through a brick archway.

'Ah, now there I'm afraid a confession is in order.' Matthew grinned sheepishly. 'I do have a gardener— I could never hope to maintain all this without one.'

'It's lovely,' said Nicole, looking round, 'quite, quite lovely. I presume——' she stood on tiptoe '— that the garden goes right down to the river?'

'It does,' Matthew replied. 'You can't quite see

the river at this time of the year because of all the foliage, but in winter it is visible from the house.'

'So your dream of owning a barge may not be so improbable as it sounds?' She looked up at him and he smiled.

'Ah, it never hurts to have dreams, Nicole,' he said, 'and the barge is only a tiny part of my current dream.'

As he was speaking he had moved in very close behind her—so close that she could feel his nearness and, as she felt the touch of his fingers on her bare arm, she felt a surge of excitement and a sense of certainty that somehow she was included in this dream. Suddenly she longed for him to take her in his arms and kiss her again.

Instead, he merely gripped her arms, held her closely against him for a moment, then released her and said, 'All that remains now is for you to meet the twins. I can't think where they've got to—I thought they would have been here to greet you. . .' He half turned to look back into the house. 'Excuse me a moment, Nicole, I'll just see where they are.'

His children, she thought dreamily, as he disappeared inside the house, leaving her on the patio. . . That was the only thing missing now in this near-paradise of his, and shortly she would meet them, so completing the picture of this man's private life.

They were looking forward to meeting her, he'd said—Ashley, a quiet boy who loved his computer, and Sara, with her passion for horses. . . Suddenly, Nicole knew they were going to be friends. . .

A call from inside the house broke into her thoughts and she turned sharply.

Matthew was walking towards the open French

doors, and behind him Nicole caught a glimpse of two other figures.

'Nicole,' he said holding out his hand, 'I would like you to meet my children. . .'

Happily she took his outstretched hand and stepped through the French doors, and because she had been thinking about them, her anticipation must have been only too apparent on her face.

'My son, Ashley,' said Matthew, turning first to a slightly built, fair-haired boy with blue eyes, whom Nicole immediately guessed must resemble his mother. 'And my daughter, Sara,' he concluded proudly, and Nicole was confronted by the female equivalent of her father, with straight dark hair, brown eyes and the same solid figure.

For a second she was taken aback at the lack of resemblance between them, but that was compara- tively easy to accept, for not all sets of twins had the same characteristics. Even the look of suspicion on Ashley's face was understandable to a degree.

What really threw Nicole, however, was Sara, who stood alongside her father coolly surveying her with a look of undisguised hostility in her dark eyes.

'I don't think I made a very good first impression.' Nicole gazed steadily across the table at Matthew.

He had taken her to an hotel on the outskirts of Hawksford for dinner, and they had completed their meal and were lingering over coffee.

'Nonsense,' he replied briskly, and she knew he knew to what she was referring. 'I told you, Ashley is a very quiet boy and most of the time he seems to live in a world of his own. . .'

'I was meaning Sara more than Ashley,' she

replied quietly, once again recalling the look in the girl's eyes.

Matthew sighed and leaned back in his chair. 'Again, I warned you, Sara is a strange child in many ways. . . She and Ashley are inseparable. I sometimes wonder——'

'There's nothing wrong with that,' she broke in swiftly. 'Richard and I were inseparable at that age. . .'

'I would like Sara to talk to you sometime, to hear about you and Richard.'

Nicole raised her eyebrows. 'You think that might help her to warm to me?'

'It wouldn't take much to warm to you, Nicole.' He leaned across the table and covered her hand with his.

'Maybe she would be more impressed if I were to talk about her riding,' she said. Once again she noticed the tightening of the muscles around his mouth at the mention of his daughter's interest.

'Matthew,' she said slowly, a little uncertain of her ground, 'do you disapprove of Sara's riding?'

'What makes you ask that?' He raised one eyebrow.

'Well, when it's been mentioned, you seem somehow. . . I don't know.' She paused, searching for the right word. 'Evasive almost.'

He remained silent for another moment, stirring his coffee, then, setting the spoon back in the saucer, he gave a slight shrug and said, 'I suppose I worry about her—her safety,' he added, then, when he saw Nicole's look of surprise, he went on, 'Accidents do happen.'

'Well, yes, I realise that,' replied Nicole, 'but most

sports are dangerous. . . I would have thought,
provided the right safety precautions are taken. . .
And these days, with those helmets they wear——'

'Diana was wearing a safety helmet,' he said
quietly.

'I'm sure it is even safer than it used to be with
the old hard hats——' Nicole went on, then suddenly
stopped as she realised what he had said. She stared
at him across the table, and from his expression,
instinctively, she knew.

'Diana?' she said.

He took a deep breath and looked out of the
window. 'Diana was my wife,' he said at last. He
was silent for a moment, staring at the table, then,
without looking up, he went on, 'Riding was her
great passion, too. She regularly rode horses from
Penny Rawlings's stables. One day she was riding a
huge chestnut hunter when it was startled by a
combine harvester—it bolted and jumped a hedge,
Diana was thrown—she broke her neck.'

Nicole stared at him in dismay. 'Oh, Matthew,'
she whispered. 'I'm so sorry. I had no idea. I know
you said your wife had been killed in an accident,
but somehow I imagined a road accident.'

'Everyone does. . .' He shrugged, then looked
helplessly at Nicole. 'I've tried really hard to be
enthusiastic about Sara's riding but. . . I'm afraid I
find it very hard going.'

'It's understandable in the circumstances.'

'She'd like it if you showed some interest.' He
gave a grim little smile. 'It would help to make up
for my lack of enthusiasm, which I'm sure she's only
too aware of.'

'It could help in breaking down the barriers,' agreed Nicole.

'I'm sorry she was so cold towards you,' said Matthew. 'I so want you to be friends. You will have to forgive her,' he went on after a while. 'I guess she will always be wary of anyone I bring home.' He gave a rueful grin.

While he had been talking, Nicole had thoughtfully been pleating the edge of her napkin; now, taking a deep breath, she said, 'You mean it's happened before?'

He nodded. 'Yes, once, and only once since Diana died.' He hesitated, and briefly she wondered if he was going to tell her what she had already heard.

'I had a brief relationship with my ex-secretary, Louise Collard—you met her, didn't you,' he asked, 'before she left Spencer Rathbone?' When Nicole nodded, he went on, 'It didn't work out.'

Nicole longed to ask him why it hadn't worked out and why Louise had left the Spencer Rathbone in such a hurry, but somehow she didn't quite have the courage.

'I think maybe I rushed things with Louise, when I wasn't really ready.' Once again he leaned forward and took her hand, holding it tightly. 'I don't want to make the same mistake with you, Nicole.' He stared into her eyes and Nicole felt her pulse begin to race. 'I also want you to be sure,' he added softly. 'You see, I'm certain that I'm in love with you and that I want you to be my wife. I think I knew it from that very first moment I set eyes on you. . .'

'Matthew——'

'No,' he said swiftly, raising his hand to silence her. 'I don't want your answer now. I want you to think about it. I'm well aware that we know very little about each other and I want you to be absolutely sure. I know I'm asking a lot of you. For a start, I'm older than you——'

'I like older men, they're more attentive. . .' She smiled.

'And I come with a ready-made family. . . It wouldn't be easy. . .so, please, I want you to think about what you would be taking on and to be completely sure before you tell me your answer.'

He loved her. He wanted to marry her. For the next week Nicole floated through life in a daze. It couldn't be true. At times she was convinced she must be asleep and that any moment she would wake up and find it had all been a dream.

She told no one what had happened, preferring to keep her thoughts and emotions a secret until she had given Matthew her answer.

Deep in her heart she knew there was little doubt as to what that answer would be. She loved him, had done so since the moment their eyes had met, and if she had her way she would have given him her answer. But he had asked her to wait, to consider fully all the implications of becoming his wife, to be absolutely sure.

The age difference really didn't bother her, neither did the fact that she would be the second Mrs Fletcher, or that he had children—the only thing that niggled slightly at the back of her mind was the twins' apparent suspicion of her—especially Sara's hostility—together with the fact that she and Matthew had very little opportunity to be alone together.

He took her out several more times during the week and, while her love for him deepened as they got to know each other better, her frustration also grew, as with the end of each evening they were faced with the prospect of either Judith and Mai-Lee's presence at the flat or that of the twins and Matthew's housekeeper at Chandrapur House.

Then, late one afternoon, Nicole had just finished her shift when Matthew called her from the doorway of his office. They had already previously planned that when he had finished work they would travel back to his house together and spend the evening with the twins.

'I can't get away yet,' he said ruefully, drawing her into the room, shutting the door and pulling her into his arms.

'How long do you think you'll be. . .? Oh!' she gasped, as he silenced her with a hungry kiss.

'God,' he groaned at last, pulling reluctantly away from her, 'I've wanted to do that all day—I've only got to catch a glimpse of you or hear the sound of your voice. . .' He kissed her again.

'Are you going to answer my question?' she demanded laughingly at last.

'Your question?' he murmured, holding her face between his hands and gazing into her eyes.

'Yes, I asked how long you were going to be.'

'Oh, yes, so you did.' He grinned then. 'I'm not sure really. . .there's a management meeting to discuss waiting-lists, and also Sister Irene Burrows's retirement party.'

'Sister Burrows on Paediatrics?'

'That's her.' Matthew nodded. 'It shouldn't take too long, but you never know with these things. Do you want to wait or go on?'

'I think I'll go on.' Nicole glanced out of the window. 'It's a lovely evening—the walk will do me good.'

'Very well. It's Sadie's night off, don't forget, but the twins should be there.'

Moments later, after she had changed out of her uniform into a skirt and T-shirt, Nicole slipped out of the hospital and headed for the bridge.

The evening was indeed lovely. It had rained earlier in the day, washing away some of the dust and grime that the heat of summer had created, and on sudden impulse she took the towpath route instead of the main road, so approaching Chandrapur House from the rear.

Tall willows lined the towpath, their long branches forming a tunnel, their leaves trailing in the dark depths of the water. She had almost reached the garden of the house when she caught sight of a rather solid little figure coming towards her from the opposite direction. As the figure drew nearer, Nicole realised it was Sara and that she was laden down with a leather saddle and other riding tack.

'Hello!' she called. 'Here, let me give you a hand with all that.'

'I can manage, thank you,' Sara replied in a prim little voice.

'I don't doubt that. I should imagine you do this quite often, but tack is heavy—I know, only too well.'

'How do you know?' Sara threw her a withering look.

'Because I ride myself,' Nicole replied simply.

Sara looked so startled that she made no protest when Nicole relieved her of the saddle and fell into step beside her.

'In actual fact,' Nicole went on casually, 'I was going to ask you if I could come up to Penny Rawlings's stables with you one day for a ride—you do go there, don't you?'

'Yes.' Sara nodded, then threw Nicole a curious glance. 'Have you ever had your own horse?' she asked.

'No such luck.'

'Neither have I,' said Sara. 'Daddy won't let me.'

'Yet you have all your own tack.' Nicole glanced down.

'I like my own things—I can pretend I have the pony to go with them, then.'

Suddenly Nicole felt desperately sorry for her. 'Maybe your father will change his mind one day,' she said quietly.

'I shouldn't think there's much chance of that.' Sara hesitated and glanced uncertainly at her, as if wondering how much she knew. 'He thinks it's a dangerous sport.'

'And so it is,' replied Nicole, then added, 'but then, so are most sports. But I suppose your father has reason to be worried.'

'You know about my mother?'

'Yes, I know, Sara,' she said quietly, 'and it must be very hard for your father, but what happened was an accident and accidents do happen, however many precautions are taken.'

'It's hard for me as well, and for Ashley, but I feel

close to Mummy when I'm riding—she loved it as much as I do.'

'Maybe you'll find your father will come round in time.'

Sara gave a little shrug, indicating that she very much doubted a change of heart from her father. By this time they had reached the orchard, where the fruit was hanging from the branches of the apple-trees like shiny orbs.

'Where did you used to ride?' asked Sara after a moment.

'At a stables near Hamble,' replied Nicole. 'It's on the south coast and Richard—my twin brother—and I used to ride every weekend, usually along the beach through the surf. I had a favourite pony called Harry, but he had one irritating habit, he used to. . .' she paused as she suddenly realised Sara was no longer beside her. She turned and saw that the girl had stopped and was gazing at her in apparent amazement.

'What is it? Sara? What's the matter?' she asked.

'You have a twin!' Her voice rose to a squawk.

'Yes—Richard.'

'Why didn't you say?' demanded Sara. 'Why didn't Daddy say?'

'Does it make that much of a difference?' asked Nicole in mild amusement.

Sara had the grace to blush. 'No, I suppose not,' she mumbled in embarrassment. 'It's just that if you're a twin yourself. . .you'll know. . .'.

'You mean I'll understand what it means to be a twin?' asked Nicole gently.

Sara nodded, and they began to tramp through

the longer grass between the apple-trees towards the archway.

'No one else really understands, do they?' Sara asked solemnly at last. 'They think they do. . .but they don't. Only people who are twins understand. . . You know what I mean, don't you, Nicole?'

Nicole swallowed and threw an affectionate glance at the solid little figure who trundled along beside her.

'Yes, Sara,' she said softly as they reached the archway, 'I know exactly what you mean.'

CHAPTER ELEVEN

THEY found Ashley in the kitchen preparing a peanut-butter sandwich. He looked up as they came in and Nicole thought he looked pleased to see her, then he seemed to remember himself, and shot his sister a guilty look.

'Where do you want this tack?' Nicole asked Sara.

'Oh, dump it on the floor,' Sara replied airily. 'I'll put it away in a moment—it's Sadie's day off, so she won't start moaning at me for cluttering up the kitchen.'

'Grandma phoned,' said Ashley, his mouth full of sandwich.

'What did she want?' Sara had been about to pour herself a beaker of orange juice, but she stopped and looked at her brother.

'Would we like to go over and stay the night?' mumbled Ashley. 'Marcus and Helen are there.'

'What did you say?' demanded Sara.

'I said we'd ask Dad when he came in.'

'How did you know I'd want to go?'

'I just did.' He munched on. 'I always do.'

Nicole smiled. 'Your father shouldn't be too long,' she said after a moment. 'He's in a meeting.' She paused. 'Who are Marcus and Helen?' she asked.

It was Sara who answered. 'They're our cousins.' Carefully she poured the juice, 'Mummy's sister's children,' she added as an afterthought, then, swinging round on her brother as if something had just

156

occurred to her, she said, 'Ashley! Guess what? Nicole has got a twin brother!'

Ashley had been about to pop the last piece of sandwich into his mouth, but he stopped and stared at Nicole in apparent amazement.

'Have you?' he said at last, as if he found it difficult to believe.

'Yes,' she nodded. 'Yes, I really have.'

'His name's Richard,' added Sara in triumph, as if it pleased her that she had found something out before her twin.

'So where is he?' said Ashley suspiciously, glancing at the door as if he half expected him to walk in.

'He's in Northern Ireland,' said Nicole with a laugh.

'What's he doing there?' Ashley's eyes widened.

'He's in the army—he's a captain,' explained Nicole.

'Do you miss him?' asked Sara.

'I do, yes, all the time,' replied Nicole truthfully, 'but it's great fun when we get back together again. We have so much to tell each other—the rest of our family have learnt to leave us alone because they can't ever get a word in edgeways.'

There was a little silence when she finished speaking, then hesitantly Sara said, 'But you're older, aren't you? What about when you were younger?'

'Well, when we were younger, we weren't really apart,' said Nicole, then paused as she noticed Sara look pointedly at her brother.

'Did you go to the same school?' said Ashley, wiping his mouth with the back of his hand, then, remembering, tearing off a piece of kitchen paper.

'Oh, yes, we always went to the same school—

nursery school first, then junior school, then high school—I wouldn't have been able to bear it if we'd been split up.'

'Louise said we should go to separate schools,' muttered Sara.

'Louise?' Nicole threw her a quick look and saw that she had gone very red.

'She was Dad's secretary,' said Ashley, quickly coming to his sister's rescue. 'And, yes, she did say that—she also said we should go away to boarding-schools—she said it was unhealthy for us to be together so much.'

Nicole was silent for a moment, then, looking from one to the other of the twins, who were regarding her in solemn silence, she said firmly, 'That's nonsense—Louise quite obviously has no idea what it means to be a twin or what the bond is like. Besides, what business is it of hers?'

The twins glanced at each other again.

'I shouldn't worry about it any more,' said Nicole firmly. 'Louise doesn't even work for your father now.'

Sara looked up suddenly. 'Nicole rides as well, Ashley,' she said, '*and* her twin used to go with her,' she added on a note of triumph.

'Don't you like riding, Ashley?' asked Nicole gently.

'It's all right.' He shrugged. 'But I'd rather play rugby. And you won't do that, will you?' he demanded, turning to his sister.

She only had the time to form the beginning of a pout when there came the slam of a car door followed by the sound of a key in the lock.

'It's Daddy.' Sara looked up happily, all discontent gone as Matthew strode into the kitchen.

He stopped and, when he saw all three of them together, a smile touched his lips.

'Can we go to Grandma's?' demanded Sara, hurling herself at her father. 'Marcus and Helen are there. Grandma said we could stay the night.'

'Did she, now?' Matthew looked up and his eyes met Nicole's over his daughter's head.

'What about your supper?' asked Ashley. 'It's Sadie's night off.'

'Don't worry about my supper,' said Matthew.

'Perhaps Nicole will look after you,' said Sara hopefully.

'Yes,' agreed Matthew, 'perhaps she will.'

In the end they prepared supper together and ate it in the large conservatory at the side of the house amid a jungle of ferns, palms, trailing ivy, and a riot of flowering shrubs.

'Did I detect a new air of friendliness towards you from the twins?' Matthew asked at last, as he finished his smoked-salmon salad and pushed his plate back.

'Yes, I think so.' Nicole smiled and leaned back, comfortable in a padded wicker chair.

'What brought that about?' Amusement gleamed in his dark eyes. 'Did you tell Sara that you ride?'

'Yes, as a matter of fact, I did,' she admitted. 'But I think what clinched it was when they discovered that I have a twin brother—that immediately put me on their wavelength. It's a pretty exclusive club, you know.'

'I know only too well,' he observed drily.

'I thought you might have told them.'

He shook his head. 'No, I hadn't,' he admitted. 'I suppose I was a bit annoyed with them for their unfriendliness towards you.' Then he smiled and added, 'Mind you, I can't pretend I'm not pleased now—I so want you to get on with them.'

She was about to tell him what they'd said about Louise, but something made her hesitate. She didn't really want to talk about Louise; she was in the past and surely nothing could now be gained by bringing her name up. The issue was decided for her as Matthew stood up and held out his hand.

'Let's stroll in the garden,' he said. 'It's such a glorious evening.'

Happily she took his hand and, as she allowed him to lead her out of the conservatory, she firmly pushed Louise out of her mind.

The last rays of the sun were touching the garden, casting long shadows across the lawns. As they walked, their feet made no sound on the soft grass already damp with a hint of dew, while above the fish-ponds mosquitoes massed in promise of another fine day to come.

'How did your meeting go?' she asked at last, breaking the silence and glancing up at him.

His mouth tightened. 'The waiting-list problem was far from solved, but the plans for Irene Burrows's retirement party are well under way.'

'How long has she been on Paediatrics?'

'As long as anyone can remember, and before the Spencer Rathbone opened she was at the old infirmary.' He gave a sudden chuckle. 'Irene's one of those people whose name will become a legend and whose ghost will haunt the corridors long after she's gone. Mind you, she's well loved—it appears practically everyone at the hospital wants to say farewell to her—that sort of thing is becoming rare these days and I think it's rather nice.'

'I wouldn't mind going, even though I don't know Sister Burrows that well,' said Nicole slowly, then added, 'provided I'm not on duty, that is—when did you say the party is?'

'Friday evening—in the social club.' Matthew hesitated, as if he was wanting to say more but didn't quite know how.

'What is it?' She threw him a curious glance.

'I was hoping you'd say you would come with me,' he said at last.

She smiled. 'You mean official, like?'

'Yes, official, like,' he grinned back.

'You realise that will do it? Once we appear in public together, especially at the social club, it will spread through the hospital like wildfire.'

'I know. Could you cope?' He stopped and looked down at her. 'Are you ready for that?'

Nicole's answer was to stand on tiptoe, slide her arms around his neck and press her lips against his.

'Does that answer your question?' she said when she finally drew back.

His answer was to pull her almost roughly into his arms and to hold her tightly against his chest. Then, taking her face in his hands, he gazed hungrily into her eyes before covering her mouth with his in a kiss whose very urgency sparked the desire which lately seemed to need very little to ignite it.

'Do you realise,' he said softly at last, lifting his head, 'that we are truly alone for the very first time?'

'It's not before time,' she murmured.

'Shall we go into the house?'

She nodded and, arms entwined, they began to walk back across the grass. When they reached the French doors she turned briefly to him. 'What about Sadie?' she asked.

'She always stays the night with her sister after her day off.'

He took her hand and led her up the wide oak staircase to a spacious room at the back of the house. Instinctively Nicole knew this was not Matthew's bedroom, was not the room he had shared with his wife. He was too sensitive, too caring of her feelings for that.

They stood for a while at the window, watching the sky deepen from turquoise to indigo as dusk descended over the gardens and the river beyond.

'Nicole. . .' Matthew broke the silence. 'Are you sure?'

She turned to him and gently touched his cheek. 'I've never been more sure of anything in my life,' she whispered.

He lifted his hand and caught hers, pressing it to his lips, then in a single movement he gathered her into his arms.

He undressed her slowly, each movement deliberate, accompanied by soft butterfly kisses on her cheeks, her eyelids, her lips, and gentle caresses to her skin as each of her garments slid to the floor.

She watched as he discarded his own clothes, admiring the lean, hard lines of his body, the muscles that rippled across his shoulders, the flat, taut belly, the long, finely shaped legs and the dark tangle of hair on his chest that tapered away to a point.

When he turned to her there was no disguising the

hungry desire in his dark eyes, and she felt a shiver of anticipation as he lay down beside her on the bed.

Until that moment Matthew had appeared restrained, perfectly in control, but when at last he turned to her and began caressing her once again, some of his self-control seemed to disappear.

Nicole's response also grew more urgent as Matthew's demands increased, and when at last he stretched out above her and the sweet moment of their union came, their lovemaking became wild and abandoned as they both gave way to their pent-up longings and frustrations.

When it was over they lay in each other's arms in the darkening room, and Matthew pulled a cover over them both as the slight chill of evening touched the air.

'That was all I knew it would be,' he murmured to her at last.

'It was wonderful.' Nicole sighed and stretched languorously, easing herself even closer to Matthew, fitting her body into the contours of his.

'I have the feeling,' he said after a long moment, 'that from now on, life is going to become even better.'

'I think you could be right,' she agreed. 'Even the twins seem to want to get to know me now.'

'It was only a matter of time with them—I knew if we didn't rush them they'd come round in the end. You just have to remember that they've been through a great deal.'

'Maybe I'll be able to help make it up to them now,' she said softly.

'Bless you for that,' he said, and his voice was even more husky than usual.

She slept after that, warm and safe in the cocoon of Matthew's arms, and was only awakened several hours later, when it was quite dark, by the feel of his hand on her breast, reawakening her desire.

As the yearning throbbed inside her once more, she turned to him, reaching out for him, arching her back to receive him as once again he took her beyond the dimension of reason.

For the remainder of that week Nicole and Matthew kept their love to themselves, savouring every moment of their newly found joy in private, then at the weekend, they arrived together for Irene Burrows's retirement party.

The Spencer Rathbone Hospital Social Club had taken on something of a festive air for the occasion, with flowers on the tables, a banner across the platform and balloons and streamers clustering in every corner.

As they paused inside the entrance and looked around, it seemed to Nicole that everyone in Maternity, SCBU and Paediatrics was there.

'Whoever is on duty?' she murmured to Matthew.

'I was wondering the same thing,' he replied wryly. 'This must have been very carefully worked out. I would imagine agency staff must be out in force tonight.'

They were noticed immediately, first by Liz Buchanan, who did little to conceal her surprise at seeing them together, then by Judith Taylor, who showed no surprise whatsoever and went around afterwards with a slightly smug expression on her face that implied she'd known all along what was going on.

Others, like Mai-Lee, seemed uncertain whether Nicole and Matthew were a couple or whether they had simply arrived together and had teamed up purely for the evening.

Any doubts that lingered must have been quickly dispelled when Edward Bridgeman made an announcement that the presentation was to take place, and urged everyone to gather round the platform. As they moved forward in the sudden crush of people, Nicole felt Matthew's arms go protectively around her. Involuntarily she stiffened, expecting him to release her just as quickly, but he didn't, continuing to hold her tightly in front of him.

In the end she relaxed and leaned against him, happy to feel the warmth of his body through the simple plain black dress she had chosen to wear, and at the same time content, if Matthew felt the same way, for anyone to recognise their relationship.

It was after Edward's speech, after the presentations, and during Irene Burrows's gruff but tearful response, that Nicole had the uncanny sensation of being watched.

Slowly, carefully, she turned her head and saw a woman on the far side of the room. A little apart from the general crowd, she was leaning against a table and looking, not at the events taking place on the platform, as everyone else was doing, but quite deliberately at Matthew and herself.

With a jolt Nicole realised it was Louise Collard. Even in the dimly lit interior of the club, the secretary's flame-coloured hair was unmistakable.

Quickly Nicole looked away. It was a shock to see Louise but, the more she thought about it, it wasn't really so strange that she should be there. She had apparently worked at the Spencer Rathbone for some time and would have known Irene Burrows well. It seemed quite natural that she should attend her retirement party.

Nevertheless, her presence made Nicole uneasy and she glanced up at Matthew to see if he too had noticed, but he was laughing at something Irene had just said and seemed oblivious to the fact that he was being watched.

When the presentations were over there was a general stampede for the bar, and in the ensuing hubbub Nicole lost sight of Louise and eventually forgot about her.

While Matthew was ordering drinks, Liz passed the table where Nicole was sitting and, seeing her alone, paused briefly.

'You're a dark horse,' she said knowingly.

'I can't think what you mean,' replied Nicole, feigning an innocence immediately betrayed as she felt the colour rise to her cheeks.

'Oh, come on,' scoffed Liz, 'you and Matthew Fletcher—you kept that very quiet, I must say. Been going on long, has it?'

'A little while,' admitted Nicole, wishing Matthew would come back and rescue her.

'Well, I'm glad,' Liz went on unexpectedly. 'I'm glad for both of you. It's about time Matthew found a bit of happiness. . . I say, talking of that, did you know Louise Collard is here?'

Nicole nodded and Liz swept on, 'Can't think why she's here. Probably to cause trouble, knowing her. It certainly can't be out of love for old Burrowsy— she couldn't stand the sight of her when she was here. Mind you, from what I heard, the feeling was mutual.' Liz paused for breath, glanced over her shoulder, then, catching sight of a couple who were passing, she turned fully for a better look. 'Looks as if romance is definitely in the air tonight,' she sniffed. 'Look at those two.'

Nicole found herself smiling as she realised that the couple Liz was talking about, and who seemed very wrapped up in each other, were none other than Dave Burns and Michelle, the new care assistant on the maternity unit.

'He certainly doesn't waste any time, does he?' Liz went on. 'It was only a week or so ago that he was declaring undying love for you. . .and look at him now.'

At that moment, as if he knew he was being discussed, Dave looked round. When he caught sight of Nicole he winked at her, then, placing one hand possessively on Michelle's bare back above the plunging curve of her crushed velvet dress, he firmly guided her away through the crowd.

'He told me I'd broken his heart,' observed Nicole. 'I'm glad to see the condition wasn't terminal.'

'I wonder if this romantic splurge is catching,' said Liz, looking round with interest. 'I think I'll go and chat up old Teddy Bridgeman—I quite fancy the idea of a sugar-daddy, and he's such a poppet.' With a wave of her hand, she slipped away through the crowd.

Matthew returned shortly after, and they were joined by Judith Taylor, who also gave Nicole a knowing smile but declined to comment, and Matthew's registrar, Peter Sullivan, and his wife,

Suzanne. A buffet supper had been prepared, after which a local jazz-band provided music for dancing.

'Are you happy?' Matthew murmured later, drawing her close as they swayed to the haunting sound of an alto saxophone.

'I've never been happier,' she replied, lifting her face and, as he lowered his head, rubbing her cheek against his.

Towards the end of the evening, Nicole visited the ladies' cloakroom and, while tidying her hair at the long mirrors above the washbasins, she heard someone enter the room behind her.

Casually she turned and felt a swift stab of dismay as she saw it was Louise. In the joy of showing the world her love for Matthew and his for her, Nicole had quite forgotten that Louise was even at the club.

Without any form of greeting, or even acknowledging Nicole's presence, Louise came to stand beside her, took make-up from her handbag, leaned across the washbasins and in silence applied fresh lipstick.

Nicole had been prepared to speak but, daunted by the woman's apparent rudeness, remained silent, intending to make her escape as quickly as she could.

She was just replacing her hairbrush in her handbag, however, when Louise spoke.

'I see,' she said in a matter-of-fact tone, 'that you chose to ignore my warning.'

'I don't understand,' Nicole frowned, knowing full well what Louise meant but not wanting to give her the satisfaction of thinking that her warning had had any impact.

'About Matthew Fletcher.' Louise pressed her lips together to blot her lipstick.

'What about him?' asked Nicole coolly, aware that her heart was beating rapidly.

'Well, I gather that you two are very much an item, if this evening's little performance is anything to go by,' said Louise sarcastically, her gaze meeting Nicole's in the mirror.

'And if we are?' Nicole raised her eyebrows.

Louise shrugged. 'Well, you can't say you weren't warned when it all crashes down round your ears,' she snapped.

'And what makes you think that will happen?'

'I told you, he will use you—in exactly the same way as he tried to use me.'

Nicole lowered her gaze, not wanting to hear any more of this woman's poisonous innuendoes.

'I bet he thought his luck had changed when you walked into his life,' Louise went on, lowering her voice almost to a whisper as another woman came into the cloakroom and disappeared into one of the cubicles.

Nicole looked up again and in the reflection in the mirror saw the sneer on Louise's face.

'What do you mean?' she asked, suddenly curious in spite of herself.

'Don't pretend you don't know. . . I don't suppose he could believe it when he found out you were a twin. . .'

'You mean his research. . .?' Nicole frowned, bewildered now by the turn the conversation had taken.

'Research, my foot!' Louise's lip curled. 'If you believe research was his motive for getting to know you, you'll believe anything!'

Nicole stared at the woman's reflection, then

slowly turned to face her. 'I think you'd better explain what you mean,' she said.

'It shouldn't be too difficult even for you to work out—think about it.'

Nicole took a deep breath. 'Matthew was pleased that I was a twin, certainly. . .but that was understandable in view of the book he's writing. . .'

'It was nothing to do with any book.' Louise almost spat out the words and Nicole took a step back, startled by the venom in her voice. 'It was purely and simply because he saw you as a possibility for those beastly children of his. . .or, put another way, he must know by now what sort of person it would take to understand them. Who better than another twin?'

Nicole stared at her in bewilderment. 'I have no idea what you're talking about,' she said in the end. 'Now, if you'll excuse me,' She attempted to pass her, wanting now simply to get away, but the other woman barred her path.

'I bet he took you to meet them on the first date? Didn't he?' When Nicole didn't reply, she swept on, 'There you are, and I bet he talks about them all the time, even mentions them during intimate moments. . . I'm right, aren't I? I bet he also rushes off to pick them up at the most inconvenient times, and it will get worse, believe me. I know, because I've been there. Those ghastly children are there at every twist and turn, they rule his life. . .'

'He is their father!' protested Nicole.

'He's obsessed with them—seems to be under some sort of illusion that because of what happened to their mother, he has to make it up to them, to the extent that they rule his life.'

'You're mistaken. . .'

'Am I? Am I?' Louise leaned closer to her. 'I bet he's asked you to marry him. No, don't answer that, you don't have to, I can see by the look on your face that he has. And you think it's because he loves you! Well, I can tell you straight, Matthew Fletcher only ever loved one woman and that was his wife, Diana. He wants to marry again for one reason. He doesn't want a wife, he just wants a mother for those children. But it can't be just anyone, because there can't be too many women who would even begin to understand them. . .with their strange, unnatural ways, their weird behaviour—but you, you really fit the bill—it's no wonder he snapped you up when you came on the scene!' With a short, unpleasant laugh Louise shut her handbag and tossed back her mane of hair. 'I got out in time,' she said, 'and if you've got any sense you'll do the same.'

With that she swept out of the cloakroom, leaving Nicole staring after her in horrified dismay.

CHAPTER TWELVE

NICOLE was shaking when she left the cloakroom and made her way back to her table. It was not so much the things Louise had said, although the implications behind her words were bad enough, it was the way she had said them. There had been so much venom in her that there was no way Nicole could go on regarding the woman's reactions as merely a case of sour grapes.

She sat down in her chair, took a large sip of her drink and tried desperately to recall exactly what Louise had said. The problem was that most of it had a ring of truth about it, though at first Nicole hadn't paid too much attention. What did stick in her mind, however, was the woman's parting shot— that Matthew didn't really want a wife, only a mother for the twins.

Something seemed to twist in her chest and, glancing up sharply, she realised that Matthew was watching her closely.

He leaned forward and raised his voice so as to be heard above the sound of the band. 'Are you all right?' He was frowning.

'Yes, fine,' she lied, mouthing the words, not trusting her voice.

Matthew looked far from convinced. 'Shall we go?' He also mouthed the words.

Nicole hesitated. Go? Go where? Half an hour ago she would have jumped at the suggestion—

anything to be alone with Matthew. Now, she knew she needed time to think.

He must have noticed her hesitation but, before he was able to comment, the strains of the music died away and an announcement came over the public address system.

'Is Mr Fletcher in the club? Would Mr Matthew Fletcher please phone the maternity unit?'

Matthew stood up. 'Don't go away.' He stared down at her, obviously concerned by the sudden change in her. 'I'll be right back.'

Miserably she watched as he turned away and began to push his way through the crowd on the edge of the dance-floor.

'I wonder what that's all about.' A voice in her ear made her turn and she found Judith behind her. 'He's not on call, is he?'

'No.' Nicole shook her head.

'It must be someone he's asked to be kept informed about,' Judith mused. She paused, then, with a smile, she added, 'It's nice to see you two together—official now, is it?'

Nicole hesitated, then gave a little shrug. 'I suppose you could say that.'

'Well, you don't sound very sure about it. . .' Judith frowned, then peered intently at Nicole. 'I say, you're not worrying about what I said about him, are you?'

'What?' Nicole stared frantically at her, wondering what on earth she was going to hear next.

'When I told you to be careful, when I said I'd hate to see you get hurt.'

'I. . .' Nicole opened her mouth but nothing more came out.

'Well, don't be. . . I was simply being cautious, that's all, but that's me—I've always been the same.' Judith shrugged and smiled, then added. 'No, I'd say you have nothing at all to worry about on that score.'

'Really?' Nicole was beginning to feel just a bit hysterical—as if everything that was happening was some sort of surreal dream.

'Well, it's blatantly obvious he worships the very ground you walk on. . .' Judith went on, blissfully ignorant of the turmoil that had just been stirred up in Nicole's mind. 'Just enjoy it, I'd say. . .' She grinned. 'It's not every day a girl gets a man feeling that way about her. . . Oh, talk of the devil. . .' She trailed off abruptly as Matthew fought his way back to the table.

'It's Bridget Rose.' He spoke to Nicole, but when he saw Judith he included her as well. 'Looks like those twins are in a hurry to be born. I have to go.'

'I'll come with you,' said Judith quickly, standing up and draining her glass. 'I want to be in on this one as well—how about you, Nicole?' She glanced down at her. 'Do you want to come? You've been pretty involved with Bridget.'

Nicole nodded and stood up. 'Yes, I would love to.' She took a deep breath, consciously pushing her own problems firmly to the back of her mind while at the same time only too aware of Matthew's concerned glance.

There was no time for further discussion between herself and Matthew as the pair of them and Judith left the social club and made their way quickly to Maternity.

Bridget Rose, accompanied by her husband, Liam, had already been admitted to the labour suite.

'She hasn't been examined yet,' explained the sister on duty. 'When we knew Mr Fletcher was on the premises we decided to wait.'

'Well, I'm here now,' replied Matthew. 'Give me a few minutes and I'll be ready. Judith, why don't you and Nicole go and see Bridget? That is——' he glanced at the relief nurse '—if Sister, here, doesn't mind.'

'Of course not—Mrs Rose has already been complaining that she doesn't know any of the staff on duty tonight.'

Judith laughed. 'Come on, Nicole, let's go and put that right.'

While Matthew disappeared briefly to his consulting-room, Nicole followed Judith into the labour suite.

Bridget Rose was lying on the bed and quite obviously, from her expression and the awkward position of her swollen body, was in great discomfort. She looked up as they came into the room and immediately an expression of relief spread over her face. 'Oh, thank the Lord,' she exclaimed. 'I was beginning to think I'd been abandoned.'

'As if we would,' said Judith. 'Look, Nicole's here and Mr Fletcher has arrived as well.'

'Ah, my prayers have been answered.' Bridget gave a great sigh and leaned back against her pillows.

'Didn't I keep telling you all would be well?' Her husband spoke soothingly in his soft Irish accent, but the look he flashed Judith and Nicole was quite definitely one of relief.

'I think these babies of mine are impatient to be born.' Bridget clutched Liam's hand tightly.

'Then we mustn't keep them waiting any longer,' said Judith.

They all looked up as Matthew, in his unhurried way, strolled into the room.

'Ah, Mr Fletcher.' Bridget's eyes filled with tears. 'They've only been hanging on for you, and that's the truth. Now you're here we can get on with the job.'

The light-hearted joking and banter went on throughout Matthew's examination, then, when he had finished, he peeled off his surgical gloves and sat beside Bridget on the bed, taking one of her hands in both of his.

'Bridget, my love,' he said gently, 'you're going to need a bit of help here.'

'Is it the forceps you're meaning?' Her expression grew anxious.

'It's a little more than forceps,' replied Matthew firmly. 'You've two strong healthy babies in there clamouring to get out, but it seems that neither is going to give way to the other—so that is where we can step in to help.'

'You mean a Caesarean, don't you?' Bridget's eyes filled with tears again and Liam began to look anxious.

'Yes, I do,' replied Matthew.

'But—but. . .' Bridget gulped and wiped her eyes with a tissue. 'I wanted. . . I so wanted. . .'

'I know,' he said gently, massaging her hand between his. 'I know what you wanted, Bridget, and if there was any way I could allow that, I would. You know that. But what I want more than anything, is the best possible treatment for the health and well-being of yourself and your twins, and the only way I can guarantee that is if you have a Caesarean section.'

'Will you do it?' Bridget's eyes had grown enormous.

'Of course.'

'And. . . Nicole and Sister Taylor. . .can they be there too?'

'Well, they aren't on duty. . .' As he spoke Matthew turned and looked over his shoulder. Briefly his eyes met Nicole's and she nodded.

'I'll clear it with the staff,' replied Judith crisply. 'I shouldn't imagine there'll be any opposition—in fact, I expect they'll be only too pleased for the help.'

'In that case——' Matthew stood up '—I suggest we all go and get scrubbed up.' He looked down at Bridget. 'We have a date then, in Theatre, in about half an hour—just make sure you keep it.' He winked at her.

As Judith had predicted, the hard-pressed staff were only too happy for herself and Nicole to assist Matthew in Theatre.

They scrubbed up and donned the theatre green tunics and trousers, white caps, masks and clogs.

Two of the agency nurses meanwhile prepared Bridget, and by the time Nicole and Judith came out of the scrub-room, the anaesthetist had arrived and was talking to Bridget and Matthew.

'I don't want to miss anything,' Bridget was saying.

'And neither you shall,' replied Matthew. 'There's no reason whatsoever why you shouldn't have an epidural.' He glanced up as he spoke and nodded at the anaesthetist, then he turned as Liam, also in cap, gown and mask, came into the room. 'Good,' he said, glancing round at the rest of the theatre staff. 'We're all here now, so I suggest we get started.'

After the anaesthetist had administered the epidural into the base of Bridget's spine and a screen had been erected across her abdomen, Nicole noticed that Bridget's husband was looking nervous and unsure of himself.

'Liam,' she said, 'why don't you come and sit here?' She indicated a space behind the screen. 'Then you can hold Bridget's hand while I set up an intravenous drip.'

'What's that for?' asked Bridget.

'So that you don't become dehydrated,' Nicole replied.

'It's too quiet in here,' said Matthew as he prepared to make his incision. 'Could we have some music, please, Nurse?' He raised his eyebrows at one of the theatre staff, who hurried away to do his bidding.

To the strains of Vivaldi's 'Spring' from *The Four Seasons*, Matthew made his incision and, while Judith drained the amniotic fluid, he talked through each procedure, carefully explaining to Bridget and Liam what he was doing.

Only once did Nicole allow her mind to wander, allow herself to watch him—his strong surgeon's hands, as he performed the moves crucial to the safe delivery of these twins—and feel her own heart miss a beat as she thought of her involvement with this man.

And then, inevitably, briefly, she allowed herself

to wonder anew at all Louise had implied, and she knew she needed time, time to think through all that had been said.

So lost had she become in her thoughts that she looked up sharply as a voice spoke her name, and she realised that Matthew had said something to her and she had no idea what.

'I'm sorry,' she said quickly, at the same moment realising it was a clamp he wanted and, as she passed it to him, trying to cover up the fact that she had been thinking about him and that those thoughts had been troubled. When her gaze met his, however, she saw he was frowning and there were unspoken questions in his eyes.

Then the moment passed and they both once more became totally engrossed in what was happening.

Only moments later Matthew lifted one of the babies from its mother's womb.

'Your first child,' he said proudly, as he handed it to Bridget 'is a beautiful daughter.'

While the second child was being lifted, Judith gave Bridget an injection of ergometrine to make the uterus contract and to prevent bleeding.

'And here,' Matthew went on, 'is your second child—an equally beautiful daughter. Congratulations, Mr and Mrs Rose.' He grinned at them over the top of the screen. 'You have identical twin daughters!'

'Do they have names yet?' asked Nicole a little later, while Matthew was suturing the wound and Bridget and Liam were sharing each other's joy in the safe delivery of their babies.

'Yes,' Bridget looked up, her eyes shining with

tears of happiness. 'This one is Catherine.' She glanced down at the baby she held.

'And this one,' continued Liam, touching one tiny hand with his forefinger, 'is Bernadette.'

'They are so alike,' said Nicole 'you'll have difficulty telling them apart. And the bond between them is there for life.'

Bridget smiled and looked up at her husband. 'Nicole is a twin herself,' she explained, 'so she knows all about it.'

'She does indeed.' Matthew looked over the screen. 'There's nothing like a twin for understanding another twin.'

His words pierced Nicole like a knife-blade and, suddenly sick at heart, she turned away.

Somehow, when it was all over, when Bridget had been moved to the postnatal ward to rest and her babies had been taken to the nursery, and while Matthew and Judith were in conversation with Edward Bridgeman, who had come in to examine the twins, Nicole managed to slip quietly away.

She knew Matthew would be surprised and possibly hurt that she hadn't waited for him, but she desperately needed to be alone.

The flat was in darkness when she got back, which meant that Mai-Lee was probably still at the social club.

While she prepared for bed the phone rang three times, and later, as she lay in the darkness watching the patterns on the ceiling cast by the street-light, it rang again.

She knew it was Matthew but she didn't answer it, couldn't answer it.

Tomorrow the situation would have to be faced,

questions would have to be answered, but tonight she felt too drained, too exhausted. All she wanted to do was sleep. Time enough tomorrow to think.

But she was still awake when Judith came home; she heard her tap softly on her door, quietly call her name.

Then there was silence until much later when Mai-Lee arrived in a taxi, the headlights shining into Nicole's bedroom as the Chinese girl paid the fare. Then, after the taxi purred away down the hill and Mai-Lee let herself into the flat and went to her room, more silence.

And still sleep eluded Nicole and, no matter how hard she tried to shut it out, her conversation with Louise kept coming back, reverberating in her head.

'And you think it's because he loves you?' she'd said, and 'Matthew Fletcher only ever loved one woman and that was his wife, Diana.'

Of course he had loved his wife, there was no question about that and she wouldn't want him to pretend otherwise, but Diana was dead. . .leaving him free to love again. . .

And he did love her—Nicole was almost certain of that—could there be any faking the passion and tenderness they had shared?

Louise had implied he was merely searching for a mother for the twins. . .but surely, she told herself, no man would marry again for that reason alone.

But had Matthew at some point asked Louise to marry him? Again, that was what had been implied.

Desperately Nicole tried to recall what Matthew had told her about his relationship with Louise, but she could only remember him saying that it hadn't worked out. . .which, surely, was fair enough. . .

But, some little demon goaded at the back of her mind, why hadn't it worked out? Had it been simply because the twins didn't like her? They had made it pretty plain to Nicole that they hadn't been too keen on Louise. . .so maybe it was that Matthew was choosing a mother for them rather than a wife for himself.

Frantically she turned over and thumped her pillow, burying her head and shutting her eyes tightly.

'When he found out you were a twin. . . I bet he thought his luck had changed when you walked into his life,' Louise had sneered.

Was that all it had been? Was that really the reason he had been so keen to get to know her?

But she could have sworn there had been an attraction between them from that very first moment. And maybe there had. But had that, for Matthew, simply been a bonus? Had the real basis for their relationship been when he'd discovered she was a twin?

And who had ended the affair between himself and Louise? Had it been Matthew, simply because the twins didn't like her? Or had it been Louise, because she had discovered he only wanted a mother for the twins and not a wife?

Nicole's head began to spin. Sara had said Louise had wanted to send them off to separate boarding-schools, that she'd wanted to split them up. . .that it was unhealthy for them to be together so much. At the time, Nicole had sympathised with Sara. . .but had there been much more behind it all?

Then again, Louise had seemed to know that Matthew would have taken her, Nicole, to meet the

twins on their first date. . .which of course he had—
that time at the house when they had been so
suspicious of her. And what was it Louise had said
about their most intimate moments? She'd asked if
the twins' names had come up. Desperately Nicole
tried to remember. . . That first time they had made
love in the bedroom at Chandrapur House. . .yes,
they had spoken of the twins just afterwards. . .but
had it been Matthew who had brought up their
names or had it been her? She couldn't remember.
And what of him rushing off at awkward times to
pick them up from somewhere or other. . .? Yes, he
had. . .but. . .damn it, he was a father, for God's
sake! It was inevitable he should do these things!

Angrily she sat upright and stared into the
darkness.

'He's obsessed with them. . .they rule his life. . .'
Round and round in her mind Louise's cruel taunts
chased each other until in the end Nicole thought
her brain would explode.

It wasn't until just before dawn that finally,
exhausted, she fell into a fitful sleep.

She was awakened, not by her usual alarm, but by
bright sunlight streaming through the window on to
her pillow.

She groaned, then, remembering she was off duty
that morning, turned over and attempted to go back
to sleep.

But once again, the thoughts crowded in and she
knew that today she would have to face up to the
situation and seek some answers.

In the end she threw back the thin sheet that
covered her, got out of bed and padded to the
bathroom.

A shower helped to revive her, then, wrapping herself in a large, fluffy towel she wandered along the landing to the kitchen.

There was no sound from the others, and she remembered that both Judith and Mai-Lee were on early-morning shifts and would have left for the hospital long ago.

Drying her hair with a hand-towel, she pushed open the kitchen door.

Matthew was sitting at the table, his hands around a mug of coffee.

She stopped on the threshold and stared at him, her heart twisting painfully. He had quite obviously been watching the door, for immediately his eyes met hers.

'Judith let me in,' he said simply, spreading his hands. He was wearing a sweatshirt and jeans and looked as if he too hadn't slept very much.

Still she didn't speak, just continued to stare at him, unable to believe he was there.

'I had to come. I had to see you. I tried to phone. . .several times. . .'

'I know,' she said dully.

'You didn't answer.'

'No.'

'Can I ask why?'

'I'm not sure.' She gave a faint shrug. 'I suppose I needed time to think.'

'And have you thought?'

'Some.' She gave an uncertain nod.

'And this thinking, did it lead you to any conclusions?' He was watching her carefully now.

'I don't know, Matthew. I don't know what to think. . .' Helplessly she pulled the towel more tightly and secured it under her arms, aware at the same time that rivulets of water were trickling from her hair down her neck and on to her bare shoulders.

'Has this got anything to do with Louise?' he asked at last.

She shrugged again and, crossing to the coffee-pot, poured herself a mug, walked back to the table and sat down opposite him.

'Has it, Nicole?' He was watching her closely again.

'What makes you think that?' she asked, sipping her coffee, playing for time, trying to clear her brain so that she could think.

'Well, clearly something upset you last night and the only thing I can think of was that Louise followed you when you went into the cloakroom. I can only assume she said something, presumably about me, that is giving you second thoughts.'

'I. . .' She opened her mouth to speak, then, giving a dismissive little gesture with her hand, closed it again and shook her head. Where should she start? Accuse him of exploiting her? Of using her? Of gaining her trust with an ulterior motive? How could she begin?

Instead, to her amazement, he looked levelly at her across the table and quietly said, 'Did Louise tell you that I didn't really love you? That I don't want a wife, that I only want a mother for the twins? Was that it, Nicole?'

She stared at him and he gave a grim little smile. 'You needn't bother to answer,' he said softly. 'I can see by your expression that was exactly it.' He paused, then said, 'So, did you believe her?'

She was stung by the look of pain on his face. 'I

didn't know what to believe,' she began uncertainly. 'I didn't want to believe the things she said, of course I didn't. . .but. . .' She trailed off in confusion.

'But she was very plausible. . .is that it?' He gave a tight little smile. 'So did she make you doubt that I love you?'

'Oh, Matthew!' Miserably she stared at him, knowing in her heart just how much she did love him.

'Oh, I don't doubt that she had a good try,' he went on, then added, 'And don't forget, Nicole, I know only too well just how plausible Louise can be.'

Nicole swallowed. 'She implied that her relationship with you ended partly because the twins didn't like her.'

'It's quite true, the twins didn't like Louise,' he admitted, gazing levelly at her, 'but I didn't know that until after the relationship was over. It was only then I learned, among other things, that she had wanted to separate them and send them away to boarding-school, but that wasn't the reason the relationship ended.'

She looked up, waiting for him to go on.

'The relationship ended when I told Louise the affair was over.'

'You ended it?' She frowned. 'I imagined Louise ended it because she thought you only wanted her as a substitute mother for the twins.'

'That's what she wanted you to believe,' replied Matthew, 'but the truth was, I ended it.' He fell silent for a moment, reflecting, toying with the mug in his hands, then, looking up slowly, he said, 'I'll tell you why I ended it, too. It wasn't because I thought the twins didn't like her, it wasn't because I thought she wouldn't be a good mother, it was, quite simply, Nicole, that I realised I didn't love her and that it would be wrong to continue it.'

She stared at him in silence, the honesty in his dark eyes only too apparent.

'Did you ask her to marry you?' she asked softly, then found herself holding her breath as she waited for his reply.

'No. Did she say that I had?'

'Not exactly, but again, she implied it.' She fell silent for a moment, watching him. 'So, did you want her to leave her job?'

'Good God! Did she say that as well?'

'Again, not directly, but even on the day she left she managed to give the impression that her leaving was something to do with you.'

'She must have made me sound like some sort of monster,' he said. 'But it was Louise herself who said she no longer wanted to work for me—no longer wanted to breath the same air was how she put it, if I remember rightly.' He pulled a face. 'I felt so badly about the whole thing at the time that I even got her the job she now has in Harley Street.'

There was silence in the kitchen, then Matthew sighed. 'When the relationship ended,' he continued after a while, 'I admit, I began to question if I could ever truly love anyone again after Diana. I even admitted as much to Louise, but then, Nicole, I met you. From the moment I saw you, I knew. . . Unfortunately Louise must have seen the way I felt about you as well. . .must have sensed the rapport between us. . .'

'She was jealous,' Nicole continued when Matthew paused for breath. 'I suppose she thought she could get some sort of revenge by trying to destroy our relationship.'

'We won't give her the satisfaction of succeeding. . .will we?' He paused and stared at her. 'I love you, Nicole, and have done from the moment I saw you.'

At the simplicity of his words a thrill shot through her. 'So it had nothing to do with my being a twin?' she asked, and her voice was barely more than a whisper.

'Of course it didn't!' He reached out across the table and covered her hand with one of his. 'Although——' he hesitated '—maybe I should confess I used that fact, as an ulterior motive.'

'What do you mean?' Her eyes widened, but already she was finding the reassurance she so badly needed in the warmth of his hand.

He smiled. 'Well, I suppose I led you to believe I was actually engaged in writing my book at the present time, just so that I had an excuse to see you, when in actual fact——' he threw her a rueful glance '—I've been doing that research for years. . . Heaven only knows when the book will get written.'

She felt her lips begin to twitch with the beginnings of a smile. 'So what about the twins?' she asked at last.

'They adore you,' he replied simply. 'And that really is a bonus. Of course I'm delighted.' He stood up then and, looking down at her, said, 'But it's me that's in love with you. It's me who wants you for my wife. The fact that you understand my children is like a gift from heaven, but it's "you and me" that is the deciding factor, Nicole.'

As he was speaking he moved round the table and, taking her hands in his, he drew her to her feet and gazed urgently down into her eyes.

'You will marry me, won't you?' he said, and his voice sounded even more husky than usual. 'Please, Nicole, I love you so much, put me out of my misery.'

'Of course I will,' she whispered, lifting her face for his kiss and sliding her arms around his neck.

He held her close as his mouth claimed hers, stirring once again those passions that had simmered so close to the surface ever since the moment she had first set eyes on him.

'I think. . .' she said shakily, when at last she drew slightly away. 'I think the twins should be the first to know. Let me dress, and we'll go and tell them.'

'Good idea,' he murmured, 'the twins should be the first to know. . .but not yet. For once, they will have to wait. . .there's something far more urgent. . .'

As he was speaking, he gathered her up into his arms. As they crossed the landing she felt the towel slip to the floor, then, as he carried her into her bedroom, she heard the click as he kicked the door shut behind them.

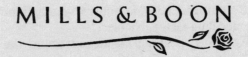

MILLS & BOON

LOVE ON CALL

The books for enjoyment this month are:

IMPOSSIBLE SECRET	Margaret Barker
A PRACTICE MADE PERFECT	Jean Evans
WEDDING SONG	Rebecca Lang
THE DECIDING FACTOR	Laura MacDonald

Treats in store!

Watch next month for the following absorbing stories:

LOVE WITHOUT MEASURE	Caroline Anderson
VERSATILE VET	Mary Bowring
TARRANT'S PRACTICE	Abigail Gordon
DOCTOR'S HONOUR	Marion Lennox

SPRING FLOWER COMPETITION

How would you like a years supply of Temptation books ABSOLUTELY FREE? Well, you can win them all! All you have to do is complete the word puzzle below and send it in to us by 31st December 1995. The first 5 correct entries picked out of the bag after that date will win a years supply of Temptation books (*four books every month - worth over £90*). What could be easier?

L	L	E	B	E	U	L	B	Q
P	R	I	M	R	O	S	E	A
I	D	O	D	Y	U	I	P	R
L	O	X	G	O	R	S	E	Y
S	T	H	R	I	F	T	M	S
W	P	I	L	U	T	F	K	I
O	E	N	O	M	E	N	A	A
C	H	O	N	E	S	T	Y	D

COWSLIP
BLUEBELL
PRIMROSE
DAFFODIL
ANEMONE
DAISY
GORSE
TULIP
HONESTY
THRIFT

PLEASE TURN OVER FOR DETAILS OF HOW TO ENTER

HOW TO ENTER

Hidden in the grid are various British
flowers that bloom in the Spring.
You'll find the list next to the word
puzzle overleaf and they can be
read backwards, forwards, up,
down, or diagonally. When you
find a word, circle it or put a
line through it.

After you have completed your
word search, don't forget to fill in
your name and address in the space
provided and pop this page in an
envelope (you don't need a stamp) and
post it today. Hurry - competition ends 31st December 1995.

Mills & Boon Spring Flower Competition,
FREEPOST,
P.O. Box 344,
Croydon,
Surrey. CR9 9EL

Are you a Reader Service Subscriber?   Yes ❑   No ❑

Ms/Mrs/Miss/Mr _____

Address _____

_____

_____ Postcode _____

One application per household.   F

You may be mailed with other offers from other reputable companies as a
result of this application. If you would prefer not to receive such offers,
please tick box. ❑

COMP395